D1550595

Across the Reach

by Cynthia Furlong Reynolds

mitten press

All inquiries should be addressed to:
Mitten Press
An imprint of Ann Arbor Media Group LLC
2500 S. State Street
Ann Arbor, MI 48104

Printed and bound at Edwards Brothers, Ann Arbor, MI, USA.

10   9   8   7   6   5   4   3   2   1

Library of Congress Cataloging-in-Publication Data

Reynolds, Cynthia Furlong.
 Across the reach / by Cynthia Furlong Reynolds ; [illustrations by Bonnie Miljour].
   p. cm.
 Summary: While spending the summer of 1957 with her grandparents in Maine, ten-year-old Betsy and a new friend hunt for pirate treasure, pick berries, and try to find a way to fulfill Betsy's ninety-two-year-old Great-Grammie's wish to return to the island where she was born.
   ISBN-13: 978-1-58726-518-1
   ISBN-10: 1-58726-518-4
 [1. Grandparents--Fiction. 2. Friendship--Fiction. 3. Old age--Fiction. 4. Family life--Maine--Fiction. 5. Maine--History--20th century--Fiction.] I. Miljour, Bonnie, 1949- ill. II. Title.
PZ7.R33513Acr 2007
[Fic]--dc22
                          2007001424

This book is dedicated with great love
and heartfelt thanks to:

My Great-Grandmother
Edna Knowlton Henley
&
My Grandmother
Esther Henley Leighton
&
My Great-Aunt
Elizabeth Henley Littlefield
&
My Mother
Elizabeth Henley Leighton Furlong
&
My Daughter
Elizabeth Henley Reynolds

Author's Note

We all have stories to tell. Some people have one Big Story; it could be about jumping out of airplanes during war, serving in faraway mission outposts, developing the cure for a deadly disease, crafting important legislation, inventing a time-saving device, or surviving a disaster. But the great majority of us have quiet little stories that, in the telling, become great Big Stories, stories that create and explain the people we were destined to become and a particular time and place in history. Both types of stories can have far-ranging meaning—but only *if* we tell them!

Across the Reach is a little story that has great meaning within my family—and I hope it will have great meaning to you and your family after you read it.

The tale of a little girl's adventures with her intriguing great-grandmother begins 'way Down East off the coast of Maine, at the home of my great-grandmother Edna Knowlton Henley. The story sat quietly on a shelf in my family's home, gathering dust next to Great-Grammie's wedding gown, until a rainy

July afternoon in 2001, when my daughter Elizabeth and I were driving from the west coast of Florida to southeastern Maine.

To entertain us while we were stalled in traffic around Atlanta, Elizabeth began reading out loud Kate DiCamillo's masterpiece, *Because of Winn Dixie.* Somewhere in Tennessee, after she finished the magical, quiet story about a little girl's coming-of-age, Elizabeth fell asleep and I began to wonder if an event in my life had the same level of meaning.

Flash! A picture popped into my head. I was a tiny little girl with brown eyes and brown hair rocking her doll baby in a tiny little chair in a shadowy upstairs bedroom. Beside me, rocking in a slightly larger chair, was a very tiny, very old lady with brown eyes and long white hair. She, too, was clutching a doll, and she was softly humming a nameless tune. Over and over again....

Passing through more than four decades of memories in the blink of an eye, I was once again a visitor in my grandparents' home in South Portland, Maine, tiptoeing past a shadowy, spooky little bedroom where my great-grandmother rocked and rocked and rocked. Once again, I could smell Grammie's molasses cookies and the bouquets of lilies of the valley, lilacs, and mock orange that filled her house. I could hear Papa playing *Pirates of Penzance* tunes on the old upright piano in the corner of the dining room overlooking Grammie's gardens and watch the shadow of a little girl dancing to the music. Again, I felt shivers of excitement and awe when two policemen returned my runaway great-grandmother in the middle of the night. Weeks later, on a moonlit night, I shivered when I saw Great-Grammie Henley bathed in moonlight, sitting in a boat parked in Mr. Sullivan's driveway, believing that at last she was returning to her beloved island.

6

Several days after my trip with my daughter ended, I shared the memories with my mother. She gazed out her windows at her own garden (filled with flowering grandchildren from Grammie's gardens), then whispered, "I wonder what would have happened if we had taken her back to the island?"

Flash! With her words, the shadowy outline of *Across the Reach* popped into my mind.

It has taken me nearly six years to love it, polish it, and perfect it. Sending my final manuscript to my publisher is like watching my child head off to college. I send them both with great love and great hopes for success in the big world, but secretly I long to have these precious people back in the safety and obscurity of a warm, loving home.

Now, a question for you! Which of your many stories should *you* tell? What beloved—or not-so-beloved—people, places, and events deserve to live once again—and forever after?

Stories are magical creations whose people and places take on a new life with each retelling. Fix yourself a cup of hot chocolate or a glass of Kool-Aid, sit down in your favorite reading place, and let me introduce you to my family and our beautiful home state of Maine.

Come with me across the Reach....

Cynthia Furlong Reynolds
February 2007

Across the Reach

Chapter 1

The summer I turned eleven years old I discovered that I had a heart—and that it worked. Not just for beating and pumping, but for more important things.

That was last summer, the summer of 1957, when I left the city and went far away, to stay with my grandparents and my great-grandmother in an old gray-shingled house that looks out over the ocean.

My parents are archeologists, which means that they are scientists who dig in the dirt to find the bones of old people—and I mean *old*. Some of the bones they find are more than a million years old. They bring them back to the museum laboratory near our apartment in Chicago to study them.

Last spring they explained in their calm, scientist-type voices that a very old and very exciting skull had been discovered in a country in Africa, halfway around the world from Chicago. They would be working over there all summer to see if they could find more bones, and they would be sending me to Maine.

I decided to be scientific in pointing out something important. "There are old bones buried here in the United States! You can take me with you to help you dig them! I've *always* wanted to go digging bones with you!"

"It's not that simple, honey," Daddy said. "This is a very important scientific discovery and we need to be there to help. There won't be another little girl for miles around and we'll be too busy to keep our eyes on you."

"Besides," Mom added, "your grandparents have wanted you to visit them for a long time."

I loved my grandparents, but I didn't want to spend all summer with very old people in a very old house in a very old town on the coast of Maine.

"There's nothing to do there!" I shouted, forgetting my scientist-type voice. "All of my friends are going to horseback-riding camp or staying at a lake with their families. Or they're taking ballet lessons or driving out to see the Grand Canyon."

I saved the most important argument for last. I dropped my voice to a whisper and said, "I don't want to go there because I'm afraid of Great-Grammie Henley. I think she's a *witch*!"

But my parents thought that sending me to Maine was fair. And they didn't think that my great-grandmother was a witch. So they loaned our orange-and-black cat Eli to a lady who had mice in her kitchen, sent our basset hound Ebenweezer to friends who live on a farm, pinned my name on my shirt—just like I was a kindergartner!—and put me on a train headed east with a college kid to watch over me.

Chapter 2

"Welcome to Maine! I can't tell you how *happy* I am to see you, Betsy," my grandfather said with a big, wide smile when he met me at the train station. "It makes old people feel young again when they have someone to play with."

He gave me a bear hug and tickled my cheek with his white mustache, just like he used to do when I was little. "Oh, Papa!" I said, trying not to smile.

In Chicago, most of my friends call their grandparents "Grandpa" and "Grandma," but in Maine, there are only Grammies, no Nanas, Mimis, or Grandmas, and most people call grandfathers "Grampie" or "Papa." I have the "Papa" variety.

My Papa is a tall man with broad shoulders, a broadening waist, and a big, broad smile that sometimes hides under his white mustache. I know from old pictures that he used to have thick, black hair, but it's all white now. My mother told me once that Papa's grandmother was a Penobscot Indian princess and he must look at least a little like her. He has black eyes, very tan skin, and he stands as straight as the wooden Indian that guards the door of his barbershop—but Papa is a lot more huggable. He has big hands and a big heart.

"Papa, where is Grammie?"

"She's home watching your great-grandmother, who needs a lot of watching these days."

"How old is Great-Grammie Henley?" I asked.

My grandfather looked at me, smiled, winked, and said, "She's ninety-two years old and it seems she's been ninety-two years old for ninety-two years!"

He left me to think about that while he went to get my suitcase and trunk.

* * *

The ride to the old house with the gray shingles can take twenty minutes from the train station, unless you take the roads my grandfather and I take in his big old gray Studebaker car, which smells like leather and pipe smoke and my grandmother's favorite perfume.

We stopped to watch construction crews painting traffic lines on the bridge that stretches between Portland and South Portland, counted the big ships docked in the harbor, ate ice-cream cones at the Dairy De-Lite, stuck our feet in the icy cold waters at Willard Beach, hugged my great-aunt Elizabeth in the big house on Scammon Street, petted a puppy named Barney who was walking a little boy past her house, checked out two armfuls of books from the library, and stocked up on snacks in the little Red & White supermarket around the corner—"just in case your Grammie forgot anything," Papa said with a wink.

When it seemed to be getting pretty close to suppertime, we finally found the driveway on Shawmut Street.

"Where have you *been*? I've waited too long to see my granddaughter!" Grammie said with a big smile as soon as the screen door slapped shut behind us and we stepped into the kitchen. Wiping her hands on her pink-and-white checked apron, she reached out for hugs and kisses.

"We've been supervising people and places and things," Papa said as he carried my suitcase, trunk, and book bag up the stairs to the bedroom that looks over Grammie's gardens.

"Yeah! We can't leave all the hard work for President Eisenhower. We heard he was kind of busy!" I added with a smile at Papa.

As soon as she finished kissing me, Grammie stepped back to hold me at her arms' length and look at me. The first things you notice about my grandmother are short silvery curls, a smiley face, and the way her blue eyes shine behind wire glasses. Next, you notice how huggable she is, with soft spots in all the right places. Then you notice her laugh, which sounds like silvery bells. Like most grandmothers in 1957, she usually wears a housedress covered with a gingham apron, stockings, and the black high-heeled tie shoes she half-laughingly calls "old lady shoes."

After checking to make sure that she looked just the same, I suddenly realized there were hot molasses cookies somewhere nearby. The spicy smell made my nose crinkle and my mouth water. Then I caught a whiff of lilacs, mock orange, and lilies of the valley, which seemed to fill pots and vases everywhere. I think of Grammie every time I smell baking spices and flowers and I always will, even if I live to be ninety-two years old, like my great-grandmother.

"Ayuh. Good," she said, after inspecting me. (I'll tell you this, just in case you don't know for some reason: people in Maine say "Ayuh" instead of "Yes" and they talk a different way from other people. That's called an accent.) Then, as if she'd said too much, she turned her head and wiped her eyes with the corner of her apron. She must've had a piece of dust or something in them.

"Come upstairs and kiss your Great-Grammie Henley. She'll be so glad to see you," Grammie said, once the looking, smiling, smelling, hugging, kissing, and wiping were done.

That was just what I *didn't* want to do, more than anything else in the world. I didn't want to climb those stairs. I didn't want to see my great-grandmother. I hadn't been lying when I told my parents that she scared me.

"Maybe she's asleep," I said.

"No, she's awake."

"Maybe she doesn't want to be disturbed," I said.

"No, she loves company."

"Maybe I should unpack first," I said.

"You can see her on the way to your suitcases. You wouldn't want her to think that you weren't happy to see her, would you?" Grammie asked, marching me up the back stairs of the old house.

But I *wasn't* happy to see her! I was *scared* to see her! She'd never done anything bad to me. Or said anything bad to me. It was just that she was so old. And so odd. None of my friends had any great-grandmothers like her. Now that I think about it, none of my friends had great-grandmothers.

In my earliest memory, I am sitting in a little rocking chair beside Great-Grammie Henley while the two of us rock our dolls. She is singing a funny little song over and over again. It feels as though we are sisters, one little and one littler. That didn't seem odd to me then, but it did when I grew up and thought about it.

* * *

At the top of the stairs, I took a deep breath and held it for as long as I could, partly because I was afraid and partly because that room smelled funny, different from the rest of the house. It smelled *old* and sad, somehow.

"Mama, your great-granddaughter has come to see you— Eliza's girl," Grammie announced, nudging me into the tiny room with her hands on my shoulders. "This is Betsy—Elizabeth Henley Sherman, don't you know?—and she'll be here visiting us all summer. Isn't that wonderful?"

After those words, she dropped her hands from my shoulders and turned back down the stairs.

I was left alone with someone who could be a witch.

Chapter 3

The room was just like a room in a nightmare: tiny, shadowy, spooky, and rimmed in dark woodwork. About a million years ago, it had been my mother's nursery. When Mom was a baby, Grammie had wallpapered the room with tiny roses that twined over the walls and ceiling. The flowers might have been bright, cheerful reds and pinks once upon a time, but now they had faded and nearly disappeared into the shadows. "I can't bring myself to change the wallpaper because it always reminds me of how happy I was when my little girl was born," I heard Grammie tell Great-Aunt Elizabeth once.

The tiny room held only a few things: a small, low, old-fashioned child's bed; a bureau with a few pictures in silver frames and a set of silver combs and brushes engraved with the initials EKH (which stand for Edna Knowlton Henley); a vase of lilies of the valley sitting on the window sill; and those two worn rocking chairs that I remembered, one small and one smaller.

Sitting in the tiny rocker was a floppy, faded cloth doll whose painted porcelain face had been worn away by love long ago.

The bigger chair was turned toward the window, so all I could see was the back of a bigger doll-like figure in a white dress, hunched and rocking.

Rocking…

Rocking…

I could also see two small, very brown, very old hands gripping the arms of the chair so hard that the knotted knuckles had turned white.

"Hello, Great-Grammie Henley," I whispered, with all the courage that I had.

Slowly…

So slowly…

Ever so slowly…

She turned toward me.

It was like watching a horror movie in slow motion. The longer I waited for her to turn, the tighter my stomach got. I stopped breathing, I think. My mouth felt like it was full of sand. I had to hold onto the doorknob so I wouldn't run away.

And that was before I saw her face!

My mind plays funny tricks on me sometimes. Even though I knew my great-grandmother was a gazillion years old, I almost expected to see a young face to match the girl-sized body curled in the rocking chair. I knew better, but I still half-expected to see someone my age in that chair.

But…!

When my great-grandmother finally stopped turning in her chair, her chin was touching her chest. She slowly raised her eyes and lifted her head. I felt my own eyes pop open wider than they'd ever popped before.

My great-grandmother's face looked like the face of the oldest person in the world! It looked like a witch's mask! It looked like an African death mask I'd seen once in the museum where my parents worked!

Thanks to so many years spent outdoors in the harsh Maine weather, her skin was the color of the walnuts that my mother and I shell at Christmastime for fruitcakes. It had the same wrinkles that crisscross all over walnut shells, too. But the scary part was Great-Grammie's eyes. They seemed to be painted on, like a doll's. They didn't look real.

They looked empty.

She stared at me, but I wondered if she could see me because her face didn't change. It took her a long time to really look at me, almost as if she had to call herself back from a faraway place.

Once she managed to see me, she gasped.

I gasped.

She clapped her hands together and yelled.

I yelled.

She jumped out of the rocking chair with a funny look on her face and she seemed to fly at me—and she didn't need a broomstick.

I almost yelled again, but when I opened my mouth, nothing came out. I just grabbed onto the doorknob so tightly my hands hurt.

Great-Grammie Henley put her old, bumpy hands on either side of my face and brought her face almost nose-to-nose with mine. I held my breath and wondered what she was going to do to me. It was *very* hard to keep my eyes open. I don't like to admit to being scared, but I was scareder than I'd ever been in my life.

After a minute, she took my hands and pulled me over to her bureau. Then, the two of us slowly turned to the mirror.

One of my best qualities, my fourth-grade teacher Miss Copping says, is my imagination. My imagination was working hard now—and, suddenly, it didn't seem like a very good quality to have. I was scared to death. I almost expected to see my face look just like hers when I peeked into the mirror. When I got brave enough to glance at myself, I looked just like I had the morning I left Chicago—except a whole lot scareder.

* * *

Great-Grammie Henley and I stared into that mirror, at each other, and then at ourselves, for a long, long time. Neither of us said anything.

She was just a little taller than I was, although I was only a medium-size ten-going-on-eleven-year-old girl and she was a mother, grandmother, and great-grandmother. She had the same brown eyes that I have. Her hair was in one braid, long and white. My braids are long and brown.

I guess that Great-Grammie might have been thinking the same thoughts I was thinking when we stared at each other. She reached out to the mirror to touch her reflection. And then she touched my reflection. She touched my face. And then she touched her face.

"Erolyn," she whispered.

"I'm Elizabeth—Betsy, Great-Grammie. Don't you remember?" I said in a whisper.

"Erolyn, I've missed you so!" she said.

She started to cry. She covered her eyes with those brown, knotted old hands and she cried. And she cried. And she cried. Her shoulders shook, and then her whole body shook.

When she started crying, I started crying. I didn't know why, except that she was so old and I was so young and she was so sad and I was so scared.

Later I realized that we both might have been crying because we were so far from home, even if we were with people who loved us.

* * *

"What's going on in here with two of my favorite girls?" Papa asked a moment later, sticking his head into the dark and tiny bedroom.

Without a glance at him, Great-Grammie Henley stooped and picked up the old baby doll, climbed back into her rocker, and once again faced the window. "It's Erolyn, Libby! It's Erolyn!" I heard her whisper into her doll's ear. She started rocking…rocking…rocking.

"She thinks I'm somebody named Erolyn," I said, wiping my eyes.

"It's suppertime and you'll feel a whole lot better when you have some baked beans and brown bread under your belt," Papa said, putting his arm around my shoulders.

 # Chapter 4

People in Maine have some odd traditions, but one of the oddest is the food they all eat on Saturday nights. No matter where we are, my mother will have beans, brown bread, hot dogs, salad, and relish. Every Saturday. Once, when I asked why we always ate the same thing—something no one else in Chicago ate—on Saturday nights, she just told me, "It's a family tradition."

That night when I sat in my grandparents' kitchen, they explained that the tradition goes 'way back to the days of the Pilgrims, when women slow-cooked beans in the glowing ashes of their fireplace—or in bean holes dug in the ground outside the kitchen—all through the night and day on Saturdays so they would have something warm and ready to eat for Saturday night and Sunday breakfasts and lunches.

"In the old days, Sunday was a day of rest and women weren't allowed to cook or bake," Grammie explained.

Then she looked at Papa, smiled, and added, "It's too bad *that* tradition didn't last!"

"Your grandmother is a woman of remarkable sense who can concoct remarkably good meals," Papa said.

He's right. Saturday is the one night when my grandparents eat supper in the kitchen instead of the dining room, so you really notice the good smells. Many of the aromas start at the stove, which must be almost as old as Grammie is. As I swallowed my beans, nibbled the brown bread, and tried to forget the old lady in the rocking chair upstairs, wood crackled and burned in one section of the stove, heating one oven and keeping the beans warm; the gas burners and a small gas oven on the other side of the stove were empty, but a warm apple pie sat on top, waiting for dessert time.

I've never seen a kitchen in Chicago that looks like my grandmother's. Across from the old black-cast-iron-and-green-enamel stove is a great big fireplace with an iron rod that swings out; this is where old-fashioned people once cooked their suppers. Next to the stove stands a really old refrigerator, which Grammie calls "The Icebox." We don't have iceboxes in Chicago, so just in case you've never seen one, I'll tell you about it.

White and fat and hunched over, the icebox is only as tall as I am. When you open the door, you see a little frozen metal door at the top. That's the freezer. Once when I was little and hot and not as smart as I am now, I climbed up onto a chair and stuck my tongue on that metal door, thinking it would cool me down. My tongue froze to the metal and my grandmother had to pour warm water over my tongue to unstick it. I never did that again! But I still liked peeking inside. When you open that little door, you see a tiny silver cave rimmed in ice. I opened the freezer, just to make sure it looked the same as I remembered it, and to make sure the ice cream Papa had bought fit in there.

With my back to her, I thought I'd have the courage to tell my grandmother about the strange thing Great-Grammie Henley had said.

"Grammie?"

"Yes?"

"Great-Grammie Henley kept calling me Erolyn. She cried when she said it. Who is Erolyn?"

"Who is Erolyn?"

My grandmother repeated the question and didn't say anything for a long time. Until I turned and looked at her.

"Erolyn is her sister's name."

"Where does she live?"

Again my grandmother was silent. Then she took a deep breath and said, "She died almost eighty years ago, when she was still a little girl."

When I heard that my great-grandmother thought I was a dead little girl, shivers danced up and down my back and it felt like my braids were standing on top of my head.

"My mother had two sisters and one brother who lived past babyhood. Except for my mother, all of them died quite young," Grammie said.

Well! I didn't know what to say after that. The three of us finished our supper without talking. Then, when my grandmother was slicing the pie, I asked another question.

"Why does she act so strange?"

Papa wiped his mustache and put the napkin back in his lap. He said gently, "Edna is very, very old, and sometimes when people start to get old, their minds get tired and their memories don't work as well as they should. Doctors call her illness senility or dementia."

"Dee— what?" I asked.

"It's a big word, but it means an illness of the mind. Scientists and doctors don't understand what causes it or what they can do to prevent it, but they're working hard to discover a cure. Whatever causes memory loss, it's something your great-grandmother can't help. And we can't help. We just need to love her and be patient with her. We need to remember the way she used to be."

"Sometimes it seems to me as though her mind is covered by clouds," Grammie said. "On good days, the clouds open up a bit and she'll say or do something that lets us know that my mother is still there inside that strong, old little body."

After my grandfather and I had eaten seconds on pie, I helped clear the dishes from the table. Grammie tied an apron around my middle, gave me a dishtowel, and put me to work wiping dishes. In my apartment, we have a dishwashing machine, so I'd never done this before and it was kind of fun. While we worked, we made plans for tomorrow.

"Your grandfather has offered to stay home all morning with Mama, so we can go on an adventure," Grammie said.

"What kind of adventure?" I asked.

"Do you like picnics and rock climbing and swimming in cold waters and digging for treasure in the sand, the way your mother does?" she asked me.

"Yes!" I said.

"Then we'll take a picnic and go to the beach," she decided.

When the last blue-and-white dish was stacked in the cupboard, we joined my grandfather on the front porch swing. Long before the first star appeared in the black night sky, my head was bobbing and my eyes were heavy.

Even though I was so tired, my mind stayed busy all through that night. Dreams—some of them spooky, some of them funny—seemed to swirl around in my head. I saw my parents dig up a skeleton that looked like my great-grandmother's doll. I saw molasses cookies growing on lilac bushes outside my grandparents' kitchen door. And I was standing at the edge of the Grand Canyon calling to my parents, "She's a witch! She's a witch!"

I also dreamed that Great-Grammie Henley flitted into my room like a ghost, dressed in a long white nightgown. Her hair looked like a cloud around her head. She ran her fingers over my face and I heard her whisper "Erolyn."

Chapter 5

"HNOH! HNOH! HNOH!"

When I woke up the next morning, I understood the dismal cry that had haunted my dreams.

Even though I was a midwestern city girl, I knew what that sound meant. The noise was a foghorn warning ships at sea about bad weather and fog. Lots of it. And I knew what the foghorn was telling me—no adventure on the beach.

"Oh, no! Our picnic!" I cried, jumping out of my bed. I paused at the door, listening for any noise from my great-grandmother's room before I dashed through the doorway and down the stairs in my bare feet.

"Grammie! Does this mean that we can't go on our picnic?"

My grandmother was busy mixing egg salad for sandwiches and she looked up with a smile. It was my grandfather who put down his newspaper when I ran into the kitchen and answered me.

"Slow down! Slow down, Skipper!" he said. "The fog will blow out to sea soon. The wind is in the right quarter."

I knew that Papa had been on ships in the Navy a long time ago, so I hoped he was right. And he was. By the time we had eaten breakfast, dressed in blouses, shorts (me), pedal pushers (Grammie), and sandals, made the sandwiches, wrapped icy cold bottles of soda pop in newspaper to keep them cold, and loaded everything into the picnic basket, the sun was peeking through the last wisps of fog.

"What will you do today, Papa?" I asked as Grammie and I headed to the door.

"I think I'll take Edna on a ride around the cape and run some errands," he said, waving goodbye. I started to ask what a cape was, but I remembered in the nick of time that Papa meant Cape Elizabeth, land that jutted into the ocean. Then I wondered why people in Maine like the name Elizabeth so much. I was glad, though.

* * *

Although you can see the ocean from Shawmut Street, we have to crisscross several roads before we actually reach the rocks and sand at the head of Willard Beach. On the way, Grammie showed me an old three-story, pie-shaped brick building that sits on a pie-shaped wedge of ground alongside Cottage Road. Its windows were dark and empty; something about them reminded me of Great-Grammie's eyes. This used to be my grandmother's elementary school, she told me. It looked really different from Ralph Waldo Emerson Elementary School in Chicago, where I'd just finished fourth grade.

"They'll tear this school down for a park soon," Grammie said with a sigh as she stopped by the front door and looked up. "Everything changes. People don't seem to have much use for things that grow old. Or for people who grow old."

We stopped at a tiny corner store for a package of gum and a happy "Hello!" from Mr. Dyer, a gray-haired man who told me he remembered my mother buying gum from him when she was my age. Then we walked past the fanciest vegetable and flower garden that I had ever seen. Guarding the little orchard behind the big, green garden stood a grumpy-looking scarecrow—or I thought so until I looked a second time and realized that the scarecrow was a man.

"Good morning, Ernest," Grammie said cheerfully, introducing me.

He muttered something and then picked up his hoe and turned his back on us. "Don't *ever* step a foot in Mr. Macomb's yard or touch a branch of one of his trees," Grammie whispered. "He isn't fond of children. He loves his trees like most people love family members."

Finally, we climbed onto Margaret DeCosta's high and wide front porch. "This is my oldest friend—we've know each other since we were both in wicker baby carriages," Grammie said when she introduced me to a round, jolly-looking little old lady.

I had a hard time picturing her young enough and small enough to fit into a baby carriage.

After lemonade and talking, we finally (at last!) reached the crunchy white-gray beach. I ran to the tidal pools scooped out of rocks beside the sparkly blue ocean, took off my sandals, and slowly stuck my toes into the icy cold water. Slivers of ice seemed to prickle my feet.

That morning was one of the funnest I ever remember having. We built a gigantic sand castle, one that would make even King Arthur himself proud, Grammie said. We searched the sand and rocks for beach glass (dark blue and red are the hardest to find) and shells to add to our collections. We were chased by skittering crabs and we chased seagulls—or, at least, I did. Then, when our stomachs started growling, we climbed over a small mountain of rocks onto a tiny, sandy cove on the other side.

"When she was a girl, your mother always considered this her special, secret place," Grammie told me. "She came here often when she needed to think or plan or be by herself. I did the same thing when I was a girl."

"Then it'll be my special place, too!" I promised.

Another tradition to add to my list, I thought.

As we crunched on potato chips and munched on our sandwiches, we talked about the old-fashioned days when Grammie was a girl. She explained that all the big old houses that surrounded the gray house on Shawmut Street had once upon a time been filled with Henley aunts and uncles, grandparents, great-grandparents, and cousins.

"I grew up three doors down from where I live now, in the white house with the columns," she said. "The house we live in was my grandparents' home. Henleys go 'way back in South Portland history."

Early in Maine's history, when it was still part of Massachusetts, my ancestors had built their homes on islands off the coast because winters seemed easier there. Living on islands made those people good at sailing.

"As far back as we can go, the men in our family were sea captains and sailors," Grammie told me. "They sailed schooners carrying very tall logs to England; the wood would be used for ships' masts. Their clipper ships brought important people and messages across the ocean. Windjammers carried rum to trade with the Dutch for tea. My mother's grandfathers sailed schooners with four or five masts all the way to China and brought home beautiful things—china, furniture, and silks. Some Henleys sailed stone sloopers, flat boats bringing granite to cities so people could build fine buildings. That's one thing Maine has in abundance—granite rocks."

I sat in our special cove on a pile of those granite rocks and stared out at the sea, wondering what it would be like to be a passenger on one of those sailing ships looking toward the shore at our special cove. Sparkly and shimmery, the calm waters quietly lapped the beach, sneaking up onto the sand without our noticing it. A small island piled high with rocks separated us from the open sea.

The day seemed to fly faster than the seagulls swirling over our heads. Before we knew it, it was time to pack up our basket and head for home.

"This basket is a lot lighter than it was this morning," I said, grateful for our picnic.

* * *

"Your mother has had an eventful day," Papa told Grammie when we found him working in the big vegetable garden. "She's gone down for a nap."

Later, just as I was about to climb into the hammock with a new mystery book, Grammie came out into the backyard carrying a laundry basket piled high with wet clothes.

"We have clothes dryers in Chicago," I told her, as I offered to help hang the clothes.

"Here in Maine, we like the smell of good, fresh air in our sheets and towels," she told me, showing me how to stretch sheets and drape clothes along the line, snaring them with wooden clothespins.

"Did Great-Grammie teach you how to do this?" I asked.

"Yes. And her mother taught her how to do it. And her mother before her," she mumbled because her mouth was full of clothespins.

"What was she like as a mother?" I asked, curiously. It was hard to picture my grandmother as a little girl and even harder to picture her mother with a smooth face and laughing eyes.

"There never was a finer woman or a more loving mother," Grammie said, moving down the line with her colorful load of laundry. "She worked very hard all her life, sewing, baking, gardening, raising children, washing clothes, and doing a hundred other things women don't need to do these days. She established the Women's Aid Society in our church and was always knitting or sewing for a new baby, a bride, or an orphaned child. Mama was the kind of person who just knew when someone needed help or hugs or extra attention."

Grammie told me that when she was a girl, her house was always full of children who gobbled up her mother's cookies and doughnuts. "When we could get Mama to sit down and shell peas or darn stockings, we would beg her to tell us stories," Grammie said. "She came from an island Down East where pirates had buried treasures and American patriots had captured British ships in the old wars, so she had plenty of stories."

My grandmother said after a moment, almost to herself, "She didn't have an easy life. She worked so hard—you can see that in her hands. Sometimes I wonder if that's what made her memory fade and wander."

Just at that moment, I glanced up at the open window of my bedroom and saw Great-Grammie's face staring down at us. I quickly moved behind the sheet I'd just hung and wished that my feet didn't show beneath.

Then I felt badly that I'd hidden from her eyes.

Chapter 6

"Tea time!" Grammie called, as she appeared in the back-yard with a tray of cookies, a pot of tea, two dainty china tea-cups, and a glass of Kool-Aid for me. "Betsy, would you please bring Great-Grammie down to join us?"

Right away, a bad feeling hurt my stomach, but I knew bet-ter than to come up with excuses. They never worked.

As slowly as I could, I dragged my feet up the stairs. I paused outside Great-Grammie's room to find some courage. I listened, but didn't hear anything. Then I peered through the door and saw her sitting the same way I'd seen her yesterday, clutching her doll and rocking back and forth, back and forth, facing the window.

"Great-Grammie Henley, Grammie told me to invite you down to the garden for a snack," I said softly. Then I repeated the words a little louder when she didn't seem to hear.

It was a replay of what had happened when I first saw her yesterday. Slowly she turned to face me. This time I knew what to expect and it wasn't quite so hard to face those odd eyes, I discovered. I was a little surprised about that.

"May I bring the baby, Erolyn?" she whispered, clutching her faceless doll.

"Sure," I said, after a second.

I didn't like the idea of reminding someone of a girl who'd been dead for eighty years, but I didn't know what else to say. As she rose slowly from the rocker, she reached out to me.

After a moment, I took her hand. It was small and thin but very strong. The skin was dry and crinkly, like a pair of old leather gardening gloves that had gotten wet too many times. She clutched my hand so hard that it hurt and she clutched her doll. Slowly, slowly, she shuffled down the stairs in her old, floppy bedroom slippers.

"Erolyn is speakin' queerly," my great-grandmother whispered to her doll in her old-fashioned Maine voice.

* * *

By the time we reached the garden, Grammie had pulled chairs under the shade of one of the old apple trees, whose branches seemed to stretch halfway across the narrow backyard.

"Mama, look! I brought Erolyn! She's come to see me," Great-Grammie called. The smile that went with the words surprised me. It looked so…well,…*young.*

"That's *nice,* Edna," my grandmother said with a smile of her own as she settled her mother into the green metal garden chair. Then, to me, she said, "Betsy, would you please pour the tea?"

"Grammie, everything is all mixed up!" I whispered before I sat down. "I'm not Erolyn and you're not her mother. She's *your* mother! But you call her by her name and she calls you Mama."

"Betsy, she's living what some people call a second childhood," Grammie said with a sigh as she dropped into a chair. "She thinks she's a girl again, that you're her sister and I'm her mother. But I have it better than some. She doesn't even remember her other daughter, your great-aunt Elizabeth. Half the time, she doesn't remember your papa. After spending all morning with him today, she asked me, 'Who's that man?' When she does remember him, she calls him Papa, just like you do."

Seeing Great-Grammie outside her shadowy bedroom, sitting in the sunny backyard surrounded by trees and flowers, she didn't seem quite as scary. Like me, she had to dangle her feet from the chair because she wasn't tall enough to touch them to the ground.

"Mama, I want to go home," she pleaded, after drinking her tea and reaching for a second cookie.

"I know you do, Edna," my grandmother said after a moment, with a soft sigh. "Bye 'n' bye, you shall."

* * *

"What does she mean, Grammie? I thought you said that she lived just down the street," I whispered again.

"She means her girlhood home, which is Down East, a beautiful island near Acadia called Deer Isle," Grammie said, sitting back in her chair and getting a faraway look in her eye. "My father was a crew member for a yacht that anchored near her home during a week-long storm. They met and fell in love. Later, my father sailed back to court her and bring her to his home here in South Portland. Mama was eighteen years old when she married. She only went back home a few times over the years, mostly for funerals."

Suddenly, Great-Grammie turned to me, held out her doll, and said, "Cuddle Elizabeth! She's missed you, too. Talk to her!"

I must have looked as startled as I felt. I turned my eyes to Grammie and I know they must have asked, "What does she mean, Grammie?," but she wasn't looking at me. I held out my arms and took the doll and watched my great-grandmother wander over to the garden to watch a family of goldfinches clustering around a bird feeder for their afternoon snack.

"Elizabeth was Mama's childhood doll," Grammie told me. "She always kept it on her bureau and only let us play with her on special occasions."

I looked down at the worn-out doll with the blank face and suddenly I felt like hugging her. This was probably the only friend I'd have to play with this summer.

As we were talking, Great-Grammie made her way slowly down one garden path and up the next, sniffing early blooming roses, snipping off the dead heads of petunias and marigolds, and pulling an occasional weed. As she moved, she hummed that same nameless tune I'd remembered from my long-ago visit to Maine. Every so often, she stopped and said something to the flowers she touched.

"The mind is a curious thing," Grammie said, as she watched her mother's progress through the garden. "Mama was a skilled seamstress and loved to decorate fancy hats for ladies, but she can't remember what a needle is for or how to use one. She was a fine pianist, but she can't strike a chord now. She was a wonderful cook, but she doesn't remember how to use the stove. Yet every once in awhile she can recite pages and pages of poetry she learned as a girl and she recalls the Latin names for every plant in my garden. I just can't figure it out."

"We don't have a garden in our apartment. Just pots of plants everywhere," I said, regretfully. I liked the way my grandmother said "gaahdin" for "garden." It made the place seem a little magical.

"Come, then," Grammie invited, and we joined her mother.

"The root of this Solomon's seal is more than 250 years old. So is this bleeding heart ("haaht")," Grammie told me as she stopped by a large clump of reddish-green leaves and heart-shaped red flowers. "Mama's great-great-great-great-grand-mother brought the root with her when her family moved from Plymouth, Massachusetts, to Maine. Whenever a daughter married or a woman in our family moved, they took roots or cuttings from their gardens so they could carry a part of their old home—and their mother's heart—with them. In those days, travel was long and hard and often dangerous. When you left a place, you could never really expect to see it again."

"I'm glad that's changed," I said to my grandmother as I watched Great-Grammie sit down on the grass near the bleeding heart.

I didn't know then how true that statement would become.

Chapter 7

Ring! Ring!…Ring!…Ring!

I learned a lot of practical things that summer. For example, I learned about party lines. In Chicago, when our phone rang, someone was trying to talk to Mom or Daddy or me. Here in Maine, you had to listen carefully to the pattern of rings to know when the phone call was for you. Seven women in seven houses up and down Shawmut Street could listen in on our calls if they wanted to. And they often wanted to. They must have thought Grammie led a more interesting life than they did, because someone always wanted to know what she was saying.

Great-Aunt Elizabeth rang up every day to talk to Grammie, even though she only lived six or seven blocks away. My grandmother would giggle and gossip with her sister just the way I talked with my friends back home. Somewhere halfway through her talks with Great-Aunt Elizabeth, I'd hear Grammie declare, "Gertrude, I just heard your hall clock chime. It's time for you to start Henry's supper. I need to talk in private with Elizabeth now." Or, "Florence, what you think about the Sunday sermon? Elizabeth and I can't agree on what the minister was trying to say."

For the first few days after I arrived, I ran every time the phone rang and then hung around after my grandparents picked up the receiver, in case the callers were my parents. I just knew that they would change their minds and call to say that I could go with them or they would come to us in Maine, instead. But that call never came. Eavesdropping on those late-afternoon conversations between the two old sisters made me feel even sadder that I didn't have a sister or brother. I'd been asking for one every Christmas since I could remember, but so far I hadn't had any luck.

After a couple of days, I finally guessed that my parents really were leaving me for the whole summer and that they weren't going to change their minds.

Maine has twenty-four hours in its days, just like Chicago does, but the hours seem longer, quieter, and slower in Maine. Whenever I felt especially lonely—which was pretty often, at first—I would open my book bag and look at my treasures: a compass Daddy had bought me for a Girl Scout camping trip; a Swiss Army knife I got from a work friend of my parents who came to dinner and thought he'd be meeting a boy instead of a girl; my favorite books, *Treasure Island, Anne of Green Gables,* and *Nancy Drew and the Secret of the Old Clock*; a secret decoder ring I'd found in a box of Sugar Pops; a pop gun and holster that are genuine replicas of the ones Roy Rogers uses; a spyglass that might have actually belonged to Blackbeard, the salesman at the gift shop told me; a Mickey Mouse alarm clock that cries, "Hello, boys and girls!"; my summer's supply of bubble gum and the gum wrapper chain I was weaving;

my collection of SUPERMAN! comic books; my Tiny Tears doll that I've had since I was a baby. (Please don't tell anyone I brought her, though.); and last but not least, my baseball card collection. My favorite rookie is Sandy Koufax. My favorite slugger is Mickey Mantle. My favorite Red Sox player is Ted Williams. They were all having pretty good seasons at the beginning of the summer.

When you have great stuff like this, who needs parents and a black-and-yellow cat named Eli and an old basset hound named Ebenweezer? I'd never shown anyone my treasures. I'd never asked my friends about theirs. I wondered if everyone needed treasures to try to keep themselves from being lonely?

Chapter 8

Splat!

Something soft and squishy hit the house.

Then I heard it again—*Splat! Splat!*

It was a hot, steamy afternoon a week or so after I had arrived. I'd been reading in my favorite spot, the hammock under the apple tree, when I heard the curious sounds. I climbed out and snuck around the side of the house to see what was happening.

A gang of boys in baseball caps was looking up at the second floor of my grandparents' house. They were taking aim at the center window and hurling mud clumps they'd swiped from someone's garden.

"Got her!" I heard one say, as two other boys wound up for a throw.

"What in the Sam Hill are you doing? Stop that!" I yelled.

They hadn't seen me sneak up behind them and they jumped about a mile when they heard my voice. One crashed into the row of shiny new bikes parked behind them. When they turned to look at me, they had guilty looks on their faces.

When they saw I was only a girl and smaller than they were, they said loudly, "A witch lives there and we're frightening her away!"

I glanced up and could see my great-grandmother's face peering from behind the screen. In the late afternoon light, the dark sweater she was wearing played a trick on our eyes and her face seemed to float, bodyless, in the window.

"She stays indoors during the day, but sometimes she sneaks out in the dark, dressed all in white, and haunts the neighborhood!" A boy wearing a Red Sox baseball hat over shaggy hair pointed to her and shook his fist.

"She's a real live witch and we're gonna scare her away from our neighborhood," a red-haired, freckle-faced boy with big teeth said.

I wanted to say something nasty, but the way those boys talked sounded so funny. None of them pronounced their words right. Like most people born in New England, they dropped the R sound and said "doahs" for "doors" and "dak" for "dark." Though I was used to my grandparents' accent, hearing kids my age talk like that surprised me.

But, back to business. Forgetting that until about this exact minute I'd considered my great-grandmother pretty scary too, I snapped, "Well, I'll tell you something. She's not a witch! She's a sick little old lady who used to give cookies and doughnuts to kids like you once. I think it's awfully mean of you to scare her!"

"Whaddaya know about anything?" the kid with the biggest handful of mud yelled at me.

"I know because she's my great-grandmother and I live here!" I yelled back, putting my hands on my hips and stomping my foot.

48

They looked a little embarrassed when I said that, but not for more than a second.

"Then that means yah related to a witch!" the boy with the Red Sox hat shouted at me. "Maybe yah a witch too!"

"Ayuh!" The other boys moved closer to the loud-mouthed kid.

"I am NOT! And neither is she a witch," I yelled, stomping my foot again. I was so mad! "You don't know anything! And do you know how I know that? Because you don't know how to talk right. AND you don't even know the alphabet!"

"Whaddaya mean by that?" the big boy said, walking toward me, tightening his fists.

"I mean that the rest of the world says 'yes' instead of 'ayuh' and the rest of the world knows that there are twenty-six letters in the alphabet, one of them being *R*, and you're supposed to use it in words like dark and door. I wouldn't be caught *dead* talking the way you talk! And if you think that a sweet little old lady is a witch, then you must be *really* stupid!"

At that moment I remembered that my mother would have made me sit in the corner for a week for using the word "stupid."

The next moment, I didn't feel quite so brave, when all five boys started walking toward me holding clumps of mud in their hands.

Suddenly, another voice could be heard from behind them.

"Hey, Danny! Joey...Nick...Sam...Bobby. How ah yah?"

The boys stopped moving toward me and quickly turned in the direction of the voice.

"Oh! Hi, Chris," the boy named Danny said, a little ashamed, I thought. "Whattaya doin' here? Isn't it time you were deliv'rin' paypahs?"

"All done," the tall boy who belonged to the voice said cheerfully. "Maybe you should be, too."

To my surprise, the boys listened to him. They took one more look at the second-floor window and looked at the boy they'd called Chris. The boys dropped the clumps by our hedge, climbed onto their shiny new bikes, and rode off, yelling over their shoulders, "This doesn't mean we won't be back!"

I watched them ride till they turned the corner at the end of Shawmut Street, then let out the breath that I'd been holding and turned to the new boy.

"Thanks," I said.

Chapter 9

"They're not so bad, you know. They're just frightened by things and people they don't understand," the tall boy told me quietly.

He was standing next to a battered purple girl's bike that he'd been riding. He still wore the empty canvas newspaper bag slung across his shoulder and under his arm.

"Well, I don't like mean boys!" I said, sticking my chin out and glaring at him.

"No, I don't suppose you do," he said quietly.

In fact, I didn't especially like *any* boys. I didn't know any up close, but my friends' brothers were always dirty or noisy or pesty—or, most often, all three. This boy didn't seem to be any of those things, though. In fact, for just a quick minute, with the afternoon sun shining bright right behind him and his arms crossed, he looked like a kind of human lighthouse— tall and strong and quiet until he had something to say, maybe some message of warning or encouragement. Just like the lighthouse down the road.

He was taller than the boys I'd just tussled with, but he

wasn't awkward or goofy or more than two years older than I was, I thought. His face was very tan, with rows of freckles across his nose. His eyes were so blue that they looked startled when you looked at them. His reddish-brown hair was worn longer than the buzz cuts most boys in Chicago wear. Even though his clothes were faded, they were neat. I'd never seen any boy younger than my Dad wear pressed khakis before, let alone patched and pressed khakis. Those other boys all had been wearing bluejean dungarees.

What I noticed most of all was that he didn't appear to mind that old purple girl's bike. I'm a girl, but I'll tell you that I'd have been kind of embarrassed to ride that bike, even here in Maine where I didn't know any kids.

We stared at each other for a minute, not quite sure what to say or do next. Then my grandmother walked onto the front porch, saw us, and invited, "Come into the shade of the backyard and have some lemonade and cookies. I'm Mrs. Leighton."

I looked at the boy called Chris and he looked at me. I shrugged my shoulders and smiled. He turned to my grandmother and said, "Thank you, ma'am."

* * *

"My name is Christopher Knight," the lighthouse-boy said, as he leaned his—or someone's—bike against my grandparents' garden shed and sat down.

"Of the Davis Street Knight family?"

My grandmother offered him a plate of cookies.

"Ayuh, ma'am," he answered, accepting one.

"Good people! I went to school with Bertram Knight. Is he your grandfather?"

My grandmother's questions were embarrassing me, but this boy didn't seem to mind.

"Ayuh, ma'am."

"Is he still lobstering?"

"No. He sold his boat and traps to my dad."

"And how is the lobster business these days?"

"Just passable, I guess. My older brothers go out with my father in the summer, and the three of 'em aren't pullin' in what my father did on his own three years ago," he answered.

His accent was stronger than any I'd heard in Maine, even stronger than the way my grandparents or that gang of boys talked. He seemed to read my thoughts and grinned at me.

Accepting another sugar cookie gratefully, he smiled at Grammie and said, "These are wicked good!"

"*Wicked* good?" I repeated. "How can cookies be wicked and good at the same time?"

The boy looked at my grandmother with a startled look on his face and she laughed and explained. "Here in Maine, saying something is wicked good or wicked fun or wicked pretty means that it's the best that it can be. I think our old Puritan ancestors decided that anything exceptionally pleasurable must be a sin of some sort."

That explanation didn't make sense to me, but I was beginning to learn that sometimes things are very different in different places.

The phone rang and my grandmother excused herself. I was left looking over a heaping plate of cookies at the first kid I'd seen up close since coming to Maine.

* * *

"You didn't tell me your name or where you're from," Christopher observed.

"I'm Elizabeth Henley Sherman and I'm from Chicago," I said, surprised that I didn't feel shy. "In Chicago, they call me Elizabeth, but my relatives here in Maine call me Betsy."

He looked interested, so I added the information I always mention every fall on the first day of school, when you have to say something interesting about yourself. "I'm at least the sixth generation of Elizabeth Henleys and all the girls in my family have names starting with *E*. It's one of our traditions. My mother is Elizabeth Henley, called Eliza. My grandmother is Esther Henley Leighton. My great-aunt is Elizabeth Henley, called Libby. My great-grandmother is Edna. My great-great-grandmother and her mother were both Elizabeth Henleys. Once, long ago, there was even a little girl named Erolyn."

After a minute of looking at him, I added hesitantly, "My great-grandmother thinks that I'm that little girl." He didn't say anything. He just nodded.

"I bet you can't guess my favorite letter?" I asked, smiling.

"*R?*" he teased with a big grin, and I saw how white and straight his teeth were.

"No! *E*!" I said, laughing.

It seemed strange to be talking to a boy about personal things, but he didn't seem to mind, so I kept going. "My favorite color is emerald green. My favorite sandwich is egg salad. My favorite direction is east. My favorite wild animal is an elephant. My favorite number is eleven. I have an orange-and-black cat named Eli and a basset hound named Ebenweezer."

"Don't you mean Eben*eezer?*" he asked.

"No, because he sort of wheezes whenever he sleeps and he sleeps a lot, so my father said we should call him Eben*weezer.*"

"Where are your brothers and sisters?" he asked.

"Why, I don't have any! Do you?"

It turns out that Christopher has oodles of brothers and sisters, from grown-up ones to babies. "My father says if we have any more, we'll have to eat in shifts or open a restaurant," he said with a grin.

I couldn't even *imagine* a household that big.

"Is your father a fisherman?" he asked me.

"There aren't a lot of fishermen in Chicago—at least, there aren't a lot of people who fish for a living there. We don't have an ocean, you know," I told him in a superior tone. Then I was sorry because he blushed and looked embarrassed that he hadn't thought about that.

When I saw that he was starting to get up, I felt even sorrier, so I said quickly, "My mom and dad are archeologists."

"What's an archeologist?" he asked, his attention caught.

I told him about how they dig up bones of very old people in faraway places and how they study the bones in the winter. "I used to think I wanted to be either a pirate or an archeologist because I like digging in the sand, too," I confided. "But I'm a little scared of old people. And, anyway, it might not be hard on a girl to have her parents leave her every summer, but it sure is tough on black-and-orange cats and basset hounds."

Christopher looked at me hard when I said that, but he didn't say anything.

"Hello, Betsy. Hello, son," Papa said as he stepped out on the back stoop. Then he came toward Christopher with his hand stretched out. "I'm Frank Leighton and my wife tells me that you might be a paper boy. Is that true?"

Christopher stood up, shook Papa's hand, and said, "Ayuh, sir."

"Well, I'm getting tired of walking to the store for my papers. Do you think that you could swing one by here on your rounds?" Papa asked.

"Ayuh, sir."

Chapter 10

The *Portland Press Herald* is a twice-a-day paper. I slept through the first morning delivery, but Christopher arrived with the afternoon edition when I was perched up in my grandparents' tallest tree, pretending I was on the mast of a ship. I was using my spyglass to look out to sea.

"What're you doin' up there?" he called up to me.

When I told him I was looking for ships in trouble, he shimmied up the tree fast as lightening and asked, "Where?" breathlessly.

"In my imagination, of course."

He glared at me. "Around here, a ship in trouble is not something to joke about."

"I'm not joking!" I protested, and then added, "And anyway, people only died at sea a long time ago.... Right?"

He shook his head.

I hesitated, then asked, "Have you ever known anyone who drowned?"

"When you're from a fishing or sailing family, you always

do," he said, looking out at the water and not at me. "The ocean is a dangerous place."

"Who was it?" I asked, and then wished I hadn't, because his face turned red and he quickly looked away. "If it's so dangerous, why do people still go out there?" I tried again.

The tall boy shrugged. "Because that's what they know, what they love doin'. After a long minute, he said, "I guess the ocean calls to them."

I didn't understand what he meant, but he didn't look as if he wanted to explain. He quickly climbed halfway down the tree, then dropped the rest of the way. He left the newspaper at the back door and then rode off. Fast.

I didn't know what to think about that boy. I worried that I'd said the wrong thing and asked dumb questions that bothered him. But, then, I didn't know anything about boys.

And, anyway…why should I care? I didn't need a friend. And I sure didn't need a boy hanging around. I had plenty to think about and do on my own.

* * *

The next morning I was hanging the wash out on the clothesline for my grandmother when the tall boy arrived with the morning newspaper. I turned my head and pretended I didn't see him, but after he spoke with my grandfather at the back door, he walked up to me with another newspaper in his hand.

"Here. This might explain it better than I can," he said, holding the paper out to me. I looked at him and then looked down at the page, which was beginning to turn yellow. "Tragedy at Sea" read the headline. By the time I looked up again, the boy was back on his bike heading toward the cape.

I hurried to a lawn chair and started reading. The story

talked about how a father and two sons had been fishing off the coast when an unexpected storm blew up. All three had drowned before the Coast Guard could reach them. The paper said that the mother and two little girls were all that was left of the family and that two other ships had been lost in the storm farther down the coast.

The fishermen's last name was Knight.

* * *

That day was a scorcher, but I didn't go to the beach or to the Dairy De-Lite for an ice cream. I waited for the boy.

"Gee, Christopher, I'm sorry," I told him as soon as he'd parked the old purple bike. "I..."

The boy nodded and saved me from probably putting my foot into my mouth again. "The danger is something important to understand if you're going to spend time by the ocean—or even by your Lake Michigan," he said.

I wanted to ask him if the family's name was a coincidence or if they were relatives of his. But, for once, I managed to keep my questions to myself until he left.

"Grammie, did you ever know anyone who drowned?" I asked after the boy had ridden away on his clunky bike.

"Why do you ask?" My grandmother looked up from the dinner she was making.

"Just wondering. Christopher gave me a paper about three fishermen who drowned."

She told me just what the boy had said: "When you live by the sea, you often hear about tragedies. And sometimes they happen to people you know."

"Then why do people keep going out on the ocean?"

"Some don't," she said. "My grandfather, Henry Knowlton, was a cabin boy on a ship that sank when he was eleven. He held tight to a mast for hours before another ship rescued him. He never went to sea again—which is hard to avoid doing when you live on an island. But for others, going to sea is all they know. It's in their blood. They love the ocean, so they go back even knowing the dangers."

I wondered what was in my blood and if I'd be brave enough to go back on the ocean if I'd seen a ship sink.

Chapter 11

After that, I saw Christopher just about every day. His paper route ended at our house, so if he didn't have any errands to run for his mother, he'd stop to talk or play croquet or throw a ball. Sometimes he helped me with my chores or went with me when I ran to the grocery store for something my grandmother needed. I'd never paid much attention to boys before, except when they bothered me, but it was kind of nice to have someone close to my age around.

"What do you do for fun in Chicago?" Christopher asked me one day when we were hanging upside down from my grand-parents' twisty old apple tree. I'd been reading a new Nancy Drew mystery on one of the branches when he'd arrived.

I had to think hard before I answered. "I guess I read. Or watch television. Or practice for my piano and viola lessons. Or go to the park. I have a nanny who watches me when my parents work and she doesn't like kids to make noise or a mess, so I can't ask friends over unless it's my birthday or my parents are having a party.

"What do you do?" I asked a moment later.

I'd always imagined that boys would pretend to be generals and stage battles. Or cowboys out riding trails in the West. Or explorers riding canoes down rushing rivers as they searched for golden cities and treasure chests. I knew that's what I'd do if I were a boy. When I'd tried playing explorer last summer, my nanny had told me that only boys could do that—not girls. That had made me pretty mad and I'd hoped she was wrong, but secretly I wondered if boys knew how good they had it when it came to adventures.

He shrugged. "I guess when you have so many brothers and sisters around, everything can be made to be fun, if you use your imagination. We swim in the summer, sled or skate in the winter, rake leaf houses in the fall, and plant gardens in the spring. If the little kids get restless or if we have a rainy day, you have to make up games or stories to get your chores done and to keep them from getting in trouble. Having fun can be hard work," he said with a grin. Then he looked at me without saying anything for a minute and I wondered what he was thinking.

I was thinking how different our lives were. And I was kind of wishing I could have his for a while.

After that afternoon, Christopher sometimes brought a little brother or sister with him, riding on the handlebars or crowding him on the bike seat and clinging to his waist as he pumped the old rattletrap bike. Sometimes he'd rig up a contraption so his bike could pull an old red wagon with a kid or two sitting in it. They all had Christopher's reddish-colored hair, blue eyes, and suntanned, freckled face, so at first it was hard for me to tell the younger ones apart. Christopher wiped their noses if they needed wiping or told them stories if they were bored with whatever we were doing. He kept his eye peeled on them if they wandered out into the gardens, and held their hands if they needed to cross the street.

"You're very good to your brothers and sisters, Christopher," my grandmother once told him, as she washed little Amos's hands before offering him a bologna sandwich.

* * *

One afternoon when my grandparents had gone visiting with my great-grandmother and I was feeling a little lonely, I pulled out my treasures, just to make sure everything was in the right place in my book bag. I didn't hear the tires of the old purple bike crunch on the gravel of the driveway, so Christopher surprised me when he said, "Hi."

"What do you have there?" he asked.

I did something that kind of surprised me. I showed Christopher all my treasures—all except my Tiny Tears doll, which was sleeping on my bed. Then I worried he might think I was showing off, but he seemed happy to see them. He knew all about compasses and spyglasses, on account of having a father who was a fisherman, but he didn't know as much as I did about Mickey Mouse, decoder rings, Superman, or baseball cards. He'd never been to a real baseball game, he told me. He admired the Swiss Army knife, carefully opening all the tools. He watched me add a link onto my gum-wrapper chain while he chewed the gum. Then he picked up *Treasure Island*; it turns out that he knows it all by heart. We compared our favorite parts of the book and what we would have done in Jim's shoes. He'd never read a Nancy Drew book, but he agreed that solving mysteries seemed like a pretty good way to spend free time in high school.

Then Christopher told me a secret. He was working to save

money to buy a shiny new bicycle, like the ones the other boys had. "The one I ride was my big sister's," he said. "In my family we hand everything down."

When you trade secrets, you get to know someone pretty fast. Especially if they don't treat your secrets as though they're goofy or stupid. Soon enough it seemed as if he'd become a part of our family.

Still, all too soon came the moment I'd been dreading.

* * *

Every Friday after breakfast my grandmother washed Great-Grammie's hair in the bathroom sink. "Just like in a beauty parlor," Grammie told me with a smile, as I perched on the windowsill watching and munching an apple. Then we brought Great-Grammie outside, into the sunshine, to comb and dry her long white hair.

Her hair stretched all the way down her back past her waist, white and cottony-looking, just like the puffy clouds in the sky. It was as shiny as corn silk. "Would you work on her hair while I take the bread out of the oven? Mama loves to have her hair brushed," Grammie said, moving off to the kitchen.

"Ayuh," I said, experimenting with the sound of the strange word on my tongue. I know Grammie noticed, by the little smile she gave me as she turned away.

This was the first time I'd been left alone with Great-Grammie Henley and my hand shook a little as I picked up the old silver comb and brush. I was glad that I couldn't see her face. I pretended she was my doll when I started combing her hair. As soon as I went to work, she began humming that odd little tune.

"Hello!" a voice said behind me.

Christopher had come around the corner of the house and

leaned his bicycle on the garden shed. I felt like running. I didn't want him to see my great-grandmother up close. I was afraid she'd say something crazy and scare him away.

I guess I should have known better.

Christopher walked quietly up to us and scooched down beside the chair. "Hello," he said in his quiet voice.

Slowly, my great-grandmother turned her head toward him. They were on exactly the same level. She studied him for a moment with a questioning look in her eyes. Then tears quietly began pouring down the wrinkle rivers in her old tanned cheeks. She didn't seem unhappy, though. She put her old, gnarly hands on either side of Christopher's face and whispered, "Steve! Steve! You've come back to me!"

To my shock—and, I'd bet, to Christopher's shock—she pulled his face to her face and kissed him on both cheeks.

I couldn't see Christopher's cheeks, but I knew that mine were bright red. I was burning with embarrassment. If he needed proof that my great-grandmother was crazy, he had it now.

Somehow, that boy knew just what to do. Again I thought that funny thought about him being a lighthouse-kind-of-person.

"I'm here," he told her, looking gravely into her eyes.

Being around that quiet boy seemed to make people feel better. Safer, somehow. At least, that's how it was for me and my great-grammie. The old, old lady reached out blindly for my hand and pulled me around toward him. "Look, Steve! Erolyn has come back, too! We're together again!"

Just then my grandmother returned to the yard.

"Mama! Steve came! We're all here! We can go home now," Great-Grammie Henley said with a pleading voice. It was the kind of voice I'd used when I tried to get my parents to take me with them this summer, I realized, kind of surprised.

My grandmother gave her mother a startled look. Then she seemed to spend some time thinking about what her mother said.

Chapter 12

That afternoon Grammie and I picked big armfuls of flowers—red ones, pink ones, purple ones, orange and yellow ones. Big ones, little ones, branches with tiny flowers running up and down them. We arranged them all together and stuck them into tin pots and vases.

"Why are we picking so many flowers, Grammie?" I asked, as we filled a fourth pot.

"We're taking them to the cemetery," she answered, arranging a pretty bouquet.

"Why?"

"Because everyone in our family, living and dead, has always loved flowers and it's our tradition to bring bouquets to the cemetery, to dress the graves."

Odd kind of tradition, I thought. First all these Elizabeths. Then baked beans on Saturday. Now this.

Papa loaded the flowers into the back of his car along with flats of red geraniums, white petunias, and blue forget-me-nots, while Grammie went to get Great-Grammie.

Do we have to take her? I wondered. My grandfather must have seen something on my face, because he read my thoughts.

"She loves flowers and she loves going for rides. And, incidentally, she loves you!" Papa said in a gentle voice.

I felt ashamed of myself for being embarrassed by my great-grammie, but I just couldn't help it.

She came out dressed in a blue dress with a blue pillbox hat, clutching her old purse and tightly holding onto my grandmother's arm. It took all three of us to get her into the car.

"Can't we take the horse and buggy, Mama?" Great-Grammie asked Grammie, balking at the car door.

"The horse is gone, Edna," my grandmother told her.

At last Great-Grammie climbed into the back seat, her eyes wide open, as though she'd never been in a car before.

Papa drove us to Meetinghouse Hill Cemetery. "In the old days, they called churches meetinghouses," Grammie explained, pointing to the old white church across the way, the one where everyone in our family has been christened and married. He unloaded the buckets of bouquets, rakes, hoes, diggers, flats of plants, and Great-Grammie, then promised to return after he ran some errands.

We were left standing among rows of white and gray tombstones, most of them with the names "Henley" or "Merriman" on them—and many whose names were Elizabeth. I wandered around the stones, stopping to read what they said and to study the star markers that held small American flags. Great-Grammie also wandered through the clearing, running her hands lightly over the tops of the headstones.

"What does G.A.R. mean, Grammie?" I asked, looking at one star.

"Grand Army of the Republic," she explained. "Those stars mark the graves of the men and boys who fought in the Civil War. Six Henley brothers went off to war, on ships or horseback. Only one—your great-great-grandfather—lived to come home alive. That statue over there," she said, pointing across the street, to the side yard of the meetinghouse, "is a statue of a Civil War soldier."

"What's the Great War, Grammie?" I asked, several minutes later, looking at another star.

"Now we call it World War I, but back then we hoped it would be the war to end all wars," she told me, explaining that the gravestone I was studying was a memorial to her cousin John, who died of mustard gas poisoning in the trenches in a faraway country called Belgium. "He's buried across the ocean, in a cemetery full of identical white crosses, but we needed someplace here at home to remember him," she said.

"Your grandfather fought in that war, too," she added softly, after a minute. "He was in the Navy. Lucky for us, he came home."

I saw old slate stones with dates that went back to the early 1800s. Some belonged to Revolutionary War soldiers; others to sailors and captains who fought in the War of 1812. "Before that time, everyone in our family was buried on the islands where they lived," Grammie said, handing me a trowel and showing me where to dig.

* * *

"Where is Frederick? Where is Frederick?"

My grandmother and I had almost forgotten about Great-Grammie. We looked up to see her running along the aisles of the cemetery, frantically calling out her husband's name.

"Frederick is here, Mama!" Grammie called, her hand on a

tombstone, as I ran to catch her mother. "He's here, he's here," she said soothingly, when I brought Great-Grammie back to her. She put her arms around her mother and smoothed her hair.

"Did he go across the Reach without me?" the tiny old lady asked anxiously, with tears in her eyes.

"You know that he wouldn't go without you. He'd never go without you," Grammie said with tears in her own eyes, hugging her mother close.

* * *

"We're bone-tired," Grammie told Papa when he returned to us on Meetinghouse Hill. I know what she meant. Between chasing my great-grandmother and working on all the little gardens by the graves and thinking about all the people who'd died, I was tired.

"Then dinner is on me, ladies," Papa said with a smile. He pulled the car into a nearby park overlooking a little black-and-white lighthouse called Bug Light, spread a blanket over the grass, and pulled out bags from the trunk. The bags were filled with fried clams, French fries, coleslaw, rolls, plastic forks and spoons, napkins, and a thermos of lemonade.

"Fit for a queen mother, a queen, and a princess!" he said, inviting us to the blanket with a swish of his arm.

"It is, indeed," Grammie agreed, smiling.

After we'd finished eating, Great-Grammie moved closer to me and handed me her doll. "Elizabeth missed you, Erolyn," she told me. "She needs you to hug her and tell her you'll help her get home."

I looked to Grammie for help, but she was busy packing up our dinner. So, I took the doll and hugged her.

* * *

Christopher was sitting on the front steps of our house,

studying the pages of a book when Papa pulled the car into the driveway.

"Look what I've found," he told me excitedly, after he'd greeted my grandparents and they'd taken Great-Grammie into the house. He shoved the old, dusty book into my hands. "Remember what you said about maybe being a pirate or an archeologist when you grow up? You don't have to wait that long!"

The book was about Captain Kidd and other pirates. It talked about how they had buried treasure all up and down the coast of Maine. Christopher had found this treasure at a rummage sale at the church and it came from a very old house. He said, "So it must be gen-u-ine."

Sitting side by side on the front porch swing, we studied the pages closely, trying to decide if any part of the story sounded like South Portland. A sudden thought popped into my head. "I think I know where Captain Kidd could've buried his treasure!" I told Chris about the secret cove my grandmother and I had visited at Willard Beach.

"Can you go with me tomorrow?" he asked.

"I'll ask!"

To my surprise, my grandparents didn't blink an eye when I asked to go off on an all-day adventure with a boy. My parents had never even let me walk to the end of our block without a grown-up.

"I'll pack a picnic," Grammie promised.

I couldn't wait! Who knew what kind of treasure we might discover? Maybe I'd find something on my dig even more important and more valuable than what my parents were looking for so far away.

That would show them.

Wouldn't it?

Chapter 13

The buzz-buzz-buzzing seemed to be coming from far, far away. I listened to it in a dreamy kind of way for a long time before I woke up enough to realize that I was hearing the front doorbell buzzing. I looked at my glow-in-the-dark Mickey Mouse alarm clock and saw that it was 3:30 in the morning.

Who could that be? Those horrible boys playing tricks again? I wondered and ran down the hall and down the stairs. I was just behind Papa, who had managed to pull on a pair of trousers, and my grandmother, who was wearing a purple bathrobe. When Papa opened the screen door, it *creeeeaked* across the silence of the dark night.

Peeking around my grandparents, I could see two big policemen in blue uniforms with badges on their chests. One was holding a flashlight.

"Sorry to wake you, Mr. and Mrs. Leighton, but are you missing anyone?" the one with the flashlight asked.

He stepped to the side and the second policeman walked up to the front door, holding the hand of . . .

Great-Grammie Henley!

She was dressed in her white, billowy nightie, with her blue Sunday-go-to-church hat, her sweater pulled on backside-to, and her bedroom slippers. Her long, cottony white hair was blowing all around her head. She was clutching the doll she called Elizabeth.

"Mama!" Grammie gasped. "How did you get out? We had all the doors locked!"

"I wish all our police officers were as fit as your ninety-two-year-old mother," the policeman said with a shake of his head. "We found her heading down the road so fast that she almost seemed to float. Ted here has been on day shifts until recently and he almost passed out, thinking she was some kind of ghost!"

We all glanced at Ted, who looked embarrassed, but I don't blame him for thinking about ghosts in the middle of a dark night. I know I do! Often!

"Mrs. Henley made it all the way to the South Portland rose garden this time."

"That's nearly one and a half miles away!" Papa said. "I can't believe it!"

Suddenly Great-Grammie spoke up. "I was meeting Frederick at the Reach, to go home. But I came back with this nice boy," she said, patting Policeman Ted's hand. He must have been half her age, two times her size, and three times her weight, I thought. (I'm pretty good at math.)

My grandfather thanked the officers and offered them a cup of coffee. Grammie put her arm around her mother and I followed everyone into the kitchen for coffee and cookies.

"How did the policemen know to bring her here, Grammie?" I asked.

"This isn't the first time that Great-Grammie Henley has run away," she said. "When she's caught, she always tells people she's heading to the Reach."

"What's the Reach?" Gee, it seemed that I always had to ask questions. Then I remembered that I'd heard Great-Grammie mention a Reach at the cemetery.

"Eggemoggin Reach. It's the body of water that separates the island where she grew up—Deer Isle—from the mainland. Before 1939, you had to take a boat across. Now there's a bridge," she explained. "Mama grew up on a farm that looked out over the ocean."

After he'd thanked the policemen once again, Papa closed the front door and joined us in the kitchen. "Well, Esther, your mother is quite the athlete."

I had new respect for the old lady.

After I watched Grammie rub her mother's cold, bare feet and tuck her into bed, Great-Grammie looked up, stared me right in the eye, and said, "I came back with those boys because I forgot to bring Erolyn and Steve."

Chapter 14

To my surprise, I found Great-Grammie Henley sitting at the kitchen table eating a big breakfast when I stumbled down later that morning. Because I'd spent so much time thinking about Great-Grammie Henley's adventure and wondering why she'd want me to go along, I'd almost forgotten about the picnic and treasure hunt with Christopher. When he arrived with the morning paper, we took turns telling him about last night's escapade.

Christopher looked at my great-grandmother with respect, I thought. Then he grinned and winked at her when she glanced at him.

"She doesn't even seem tired!" I said.

"She looks like she could run another three miles," he added.

"All that excitement and exercise has made her hungrier than a regiment of soldiers," Papa suggested, watching his mother-in-law make her way through a pile of cornmeal pancakes and bacon, ignoring the conversation. "Her poor daughter, on the other hand, didn't sleep a wink. She can barely move."

"Gee, Christopher, I'm not sure I can go," I said. I'd never before seen my grandmother in her nightclothes during the day.

"Nonsense! Today is a beautiful day for a treasure hunt. I have your lunch all packed," Grammie said.

Christopher looked at me, then looked at my grandmother, then asked her something that surprised me so much that I fell off my chair. When I picked myself up, I had to ask him to repeat it, just to make sure my ears weren't making things up.

"Can we take Great-Grammie Henley with us today so you can get some rest?"

No! No! No!

I was horrified! I couldn't believe he'd say that! I didn't know anyone but Christopher and my grandparents here in Maine, but I still didn't want to be seen in public with a Great-Grammie who said and did such odd things. Still, I was sure my grandparents wouldn't let a ten-going-on-eleven-year-old girl and a twelve-year-old boy walk off with a ninety-two-year-old woman. Not if two grown-up policemen had been chasing her the night before.

"Oh! Thank you. But, no…," my Grandmother said, then looked at Papa.

"I think that's a very generous offer, Christopher!" Papa said, looking back at Grammie. "A trip to the beach might be just what she needs."

If I hadn't been speechless, I'd have protested. She'd ruin our fun! It was turning from a great day into a terrible day.

Well, Grammie made another sandwich, wrapped another jar filled with cold Kool-Aid in newspapers, and nestled them in the picnic basket with our lunch. Christopher loaded the basket onto his little brother's red wagon, which already held shovels, a blueberry rake, sifter, brown paper sacks (for carrying our loot home), and a flashlight. I added my compass, spyglass, beach towels, a notebook, pens (for recording our finds, just like my parents did), and a piece of fool's gold while Great-Grammie got ready.

"That'll help us tell the difference between the real and fake treasure," I explained, as Christopher picked up the fool's gold and studied it. "Scientists call it pyrite."

When Great-Grammie came down the stairs, she was wearing a sun hat and housedress. As always, she carried her purse and her doll, which we put in the wagon so we could each hold a hand. I felt like we were in a parade as we slowly made our way to the beach. Christopher and I walked on either side of Great-Grammie and took turns pulling the old red wagon, which creaked every time the wheels turned. Every once in awhile when we went around a corner, something would fall off the wagon and we'd have to stop and reload.

When we came near my Grammie's old school, wouldn't you know it? Those awful boys were sitting on the fence, practicing blowing bubblegum bubbles and trying to make their yo-yos walk the moon.

"Hi, Danny…Joey…Nick…Bobby…Sam," Christopher said casually as we walked past. They stared at us—as if they couldn't believe their eyes.

"Hi, Danny…Joey…Nick…Bobby…Sam," I said, trying to be just as casual as Christopher was—except he wasn't trying. I wanted to run away or shrink to the size of my pyrite stone. After we passed them, I swallowed hard and said, "I'll bet they swallow their big wads of gum when their jaws rejoin their faces."

Christopher started to laugh and, after a minute, I did, too. Kind of.

"You don't need to be ashamed of your Great-Grammie, you know," he said, looking at me.

Why does everyone think they can read my mind? "That's easy to say if she's not your crazy old relative!" I was feeling hot and sniffy.

"She can't help the way she is," he began.

"I love you, Erolyn and Steve," the old lady said suddenly with a happy smile, squeezing our hands.

I felt ashamed of myself.

Maybe it wasn't going to be such a bad day after all.

* * *

The closer we got to the beach, the faster my Great-Grammie seemed to walk. She lifted her head up and sniffed. I knew that she could smell what I was smelling—the salt in the air, the breeze that seemed fresher, the wild sea roses ("ragosa roses," Grammie would say) that grew along the path to the shore.

"She can move faster than I thought," Christopher said, as he let go of her hand to concentrate on pulling the wagon through the soft, dry sand.

"We'd better watch her. She ran a long ways last night in her slippers," I reminded him.

As soon as we hit Willard Beach, Great-Grammie plunked down on the sand and we took off our Keds and socks and waded out into the icy Atlantic water. We searched the closest tidal pools for anything interesting, watched a one-claw crab skitter for cover, and then I pointed to the gray cliff at the end of the beach.

"Haven't you ever seen this cove?" I asked, pleased that I knew something a native of Maine didn't know.

"We don't come to this beach often. We swim at a beach closer to our house," he explained.

When we reached the wall of rocks, my feet were already sore and I tiptoed carefully, but Christopher scrambled up the jagged rocks like he was a mountain goat. Great-Grammie stood at the foot and looked up at the top.

"Can you climb, Great-Grammie?"

Without a word, she started climbing and she beat me to the top. We stood there with the sun in our eyes, looking out at the glistening water, so blue it seemed like a carpet of jewels. I spent a couple of minutes daydreaming about pirates. I almost forgot why we were there, until…

"Wow! This is great!" Christopher said, surveying the small, enclosed cove. It made me feel good that a boy from Maine would think this hidden place was as special as I thought. While I watched Great-Grammie, Christopher carried our lunch basket and all the archeological things up and down the rocks and into our private cove. Then he hid the red wagon so no one would see it and wonder where we were.

The tide was way out by this time, so there was more beach to inspect than I'd seen on my first visit. Sharp rocks poked up through the sand of the tiny beach, which was covered with a carpet of tiny sea shells, sea glass, and a sprinkling of sand dollars.

"Where do we start, Christopher?" I asked, looking at the horizon and imagining a pirate ship off in the distance and a rowboat full of dangerous-looking sailors approaching shore. With a sigh, I realized that the waters were empty of everything but a bell buoy.

"We need to get our bearings. Compass, please," Christopher said. I handed him my compass, turned to the first page of my notebook, clicked open the pen, and stood ready to write down his words of wisdom.

After hemming and hawing, turning the compass toward north and then checking the position of the sun, consulting the ancient book about Captain Kidd, and then consulting the compass and the sun again, we looked at each other.

"My parents set up grids in the dirt with string, so they can mark where they're going to dig," I said, finally.

"Sounds good," Christopher said. He reached into his pocket and took out a ball of string. "We can use rocks to hold the string in place."

We spent a good amount of time placing string back and forth, up and down the sand, so interested in what we were doing that we forgot about Great-Grammie. Suddenly, I turned to look for her. She was in the water, all the way up to her knees and wading deeper!

"Great-Grammie! Come back! Come back!" I screeched, running into the water. Christopher was behind me, but he caught up and passed me, splashing up to her and putting his arm around her shoulder.

"Where are you going, Great-Grammie Henley?"

"Across the Reach," she said, never taking her eyes off the rocky island that floated out in the water, far offshore.

"Great-Grammie, this isn't Deer Isle! This is South Portland! Where you live," I told her.

Christopher stood quietly on her other side, holding her hand. Suddenly, my great-grandmother turned and looked me right in my eye. It didn't seem as if there were clouds over her mind today. She squeezed my hand and whispered, "Come with me now, Erolyn. We need to go *now*."

* * *

It wasn't easy, but we finally managed to talk her out of the water. By that time, we were all wet. Christopher and I had our bathing suits under our shorts, but all we could do for Great-Grammie was to take off her shoes and stockings and spread them on the rocks to dry. She leaned back on a rock that had a seat scooped out of its lap, sighed, reached for her old doll, and closed her eyes.

"What did she mean about a Reach?" Christopher asked me when we returned to the string.

I explained what my grandmother had told me about the beautiful island and the water that stretched between Deer Isle and the mainland.

"Why don't we take her there some day?" he asked.

I started to explain that it was far, far away, of course, and that you just can't pick up and go somewhere far away, but then I stopped. I had no idea where Deer Isle was, but distances had never stopped my parents from going to faraway places to dig up old people.

"I've sailed past Deer Isle with my father when the fishing was poor here," Christopher said. "But I think distances seem farther when you're on land."

His question made me wonder why my grandparents didn't take her to the island.

* * *

We worked all morning stringing the beach. Every once in awhile one of us would accidentally-on-purpose tie the other one up with the string and then threaten a walk on the gangplank. Finally, we were done. We looked at our work, then at each other, but we were too hungry to start digging, so we perched on the cliff just like the seagulls did and unpacked our picnic. Great-Grammie ate a few bites silently, drank some juice, then closed her eyes again and basked in the sun like an ancient kind of mermaid. Christopher and I gobbled our sandwiches, chips, carrots, and strawberry turnovers like the greediest of herring gulls.

"Now that we've finished stringing the beach, where do you want to start digging?" I asked.

"We have to think like a pirate," Christopher said, putting his drink down and picking up the book.

Well, we argued and pointed and paced back and forth and in the end we decided to dig where the digging looked easiest, at the back of the cove, farthest from the water. "The pirates wouldn't want their treasure to be uncovered by the tides," Christopher pointed out.

That made sense, I thought.

It looked as though we'd made a smart decision because our shovels soon struck something that sounded hollow and felt hard. We dug and dug and uncovered the neck of an old greenish-blue bottle. We kept digging and the bottle kept growing in size. It took us nearly two hours to uncover the whole thing. When we finally managed to heave it up onto the beach, it stood almost to my waist.

"Not a chip on it," he marveled.

"This must be what the pirates brought with them for drinks!"

"Filled with rum," he added.

His eyes shined and sparkled just like the waves that had crept up on us. We rolled the bottle to the water, hoping that once the sand was washed away, we would find a message in it.

We didn't, but our discovery made us forget how tired we were and we went to another square marked out with string. This time we didn't find anything more exciting than a few big clamshells, a length of rotten rope, and the broken end of a sand shovel.

"Do you think they used this rope to pull the chest?" I asked.

"I don't think pirates use blue nylon rope," Christopher said. "They probably only have real rope, the kind my father uses to moor the boat. And they sure don't use yellow plastic beach shovels for digging."

The sun had climbed to the top of the sky and then had begun to slide back down before Christopher and I decided we had to give up our treasure hunt for this day. Together we carefully half-carried, half-rolled the big bottle up the rock wall. Great-Grammie had fallen asleep again in the sun, holding her doll. When I touched her shoulder to tell her we'd be heading home, her face seemed to lose some of its wrinkles. "Home!" she chirped happily, but all the wrinkles came back when she realized we were heading away from the water. Her eyes looked empty again, as if window shades had been pulled over them.

The walk home seemed much longer than the walk to the beach had felt that morning. Great-Grammie had slowed to a shuffle. Christopher and I were dragging our feet, too, because we had to hold her hand, take turns pulling the wagon, and lug the basket and the shovels so the bottle would fit on the wagon bed.

Chapter 15

"What do you have there?" my grandparents asked in surprise when they saw the bottle.

We told them all about our first pirate adventure and Great-Grammie's plunge into the ocean.

"Was she too much for you?" Grammie asked, anxiously.

"Not at all, ma'am," Christopher said. "She spent the rest of the day sitting in the sun, napping."

My grandparents asked Chris to stay for supper and he agreed right away, telling them that he'd already asked his brother Charles to deliver the newspapers. "I promised I'd give him something from my share of the treasure," he confided to Papa. I heard him from my bedroom window as I washed up and changed into clean clothes.

"What will you do with the treasure you find?" Papa asked us as we sat on the front porch around a card table covered in a red-and-white-checked cloth, watching neighbors stroll by as we ate baked chicken, green beans cooked with salt pork, roast potatoes, stewed tomatoes, and blueberry pie.

"I'll buy brand new bicycles for my brothers and sisters and me," Christopher said right away. "We've never had a new bike in my family."

"Betsy?"

I had to think for a minute, but then I knew what I'd do: "I'll hire someone else to dig up old bones, so my parents can come here with me."

* * *

Papa and Christopher took Great-Grammie into the parlor while Grammie and I did the dishes that night. When we joined them, Papa said to Grammie, "It's been a long time since we've had a little night music."

He smiled at his wife and went to the big old upright piano that stood in the corner of the dining room. I love it when he plays the piano. He plays songs no one in Chicago has ever heard of. When I was little, he'd hoist me up on the piano bench next to him and let me pound away at the high-end keys while he played music. He told me I was helping him learn how to play duets. I realized now that I was definitely *not* helping him when I was little.

Papa ran his big, strong fingers up and down the keyboard, then started playing songs from old sheet music that had World War I soldiers and pretty girls on their covers. "Let's start with 'K-K-K-Katy, Beautiful Katy,'" he invited.

Great-Grammie stayed in her chair holding her rag doll, but the rest of us moved to the piano. After we finished singing a lot of old songs, he started, "I Am the Very Model of a Modern Major General."

"That's from *Pirates of Penzance,* a Gilbert and Sullivan operetta," I told Christopher importantly.

"I know," he whispered back. He was probably the only

twelve-year-old boy in America who knew Gilbert and Sullivan. Papa flew through the tongue-twisting lyrics, and then we all joined in the chorus and laughed at the song's funny, happy ending.

At that moment, Great-Grammie came to stand beside us. She touched Papa on the shoulder and asked, "Dance, please?"

Papa stood up, turned to my grandmother, and asked, "Esther, will you please do us the honors?"

He led his mother-in-law to the middle of the parlor rug. When Grammie started playing a smooth, slow dance song, Papa bowed to Great-Grammie, took her hand, put his other hand on her waist, and started twirling her.

A smile burst out on my great-grandmother's face and she seemed to turn into a girl, almost. I don't think I'll ever forget how happy she looked with her eyes closed, whirling and twirling in perfect step to the music. After a minute, Christopher walked up to me and bowed like Papa had. We didn't know how to do the dance the grown-ups were doing, but we twirled and spun around and kicked up our feet and laughed and giggled.

After awhile, when I was too dizzy to twirl any more, I asked my grandmother if she wanted to dance. I sat down at the piano keys and pounded out "The Blue Danube," which had been my recital piece last winter and was about the only song I could remember when I played in front of people. My grandfather bowed to Grammie, Christopher bowed to Great-Grammie, and everyone began stepping and spinning and twirling as I pounded on the keys. I played that song at least six times before they stopped dancing.

Later, just as the sky was beginning to change into dark colors, Grammie tucked Great-Grammie into bed like a little girl, with the covers folded neatly up under her chin and her doll in her arms. Then she came and joined Papa and Christopher and me on the porch, where we were watching the stars and the neighbors' lights click on.

"You've made your great-grandmother very happy today," she told us.

"That woman has more energy than all four of us combined," Papa said admiringly.

"When I first met her, she told me that she was known to have the best dancing feet in all of Portland," he added. "She might have lost most of her memory, but she'll never lose her love for dancing. She can move like a girl when she wants to. It's amazing, really."

Grammie told us stories about her mother when she was a young girl, how she had secretly dreamed of being a fine lady who attended balls every night. "She loved the Cinderella story and she told it often to me and your great-aunt Elizabeth when we were little girls. In fact, I think she always regarded my father as Prince Charming," Grammie said with a faraway smile.

I was surprised to hear that someone besides me had secret dreams. That made Great-Grammie seem more real to me than anything else I'd heard about her.

Then I wondered if I'd ever have a Prince Charming—or want one.

* * *

After Christopher had turned his bike for home, I lay in bed and thought about my day. I had gone off in public with my crazy old great-grandmother and it had still been a fun day. I had a friend who liked the same things I liked and didn't think

I was a pesty girl or an outsider. We'd eaten a picnic, found pirate treasure, danced, and sung songs. This was the first happy feeling I'd had in my heart since my parents told me about leaving me behind this summer.

I slept as soundly as that old jug had slept in the sand.

Chapter 16

I ate breakfast and dressed in my shorts and sandals long before the sun cleared the horizon over the ocean the next morning. I waited impatiently for hours, it seemed, before Christopher appeared, wearing his empty canvas newspaper bag and riding as fast as the battered purple bike would bring him. Old tin buckets clunked and clanged against each other on the handlebars.

"My mother has decided that today is the day for makin' strawberry jam, so I can't go to the beach," he said. "I've gotta go pickin'."

"If I go with you, you'll be done faster!" I offered, anxious to return to our treasure hunt.

He looked surprised and gave me a funny little look, hesitated just for a minute, then said, "Sure."

I checked with Grammie. She packed us some cookies, apples, and drinks in a paper sack, found a battered pan with a long handle for me, and waved as we headed out toward the cape. Christopher pushed his bike as he walked alongside me.

"Here's the strawberry patch. We picked here a couple of days ago," I said, turning down a lane that had a big, faded, red-and-white "Strawberries 2 Pik" sign.

"You have to pay for those berries," he said, pulling back.

"Don't you have to pay for all strawberries?"

"Come with me."

We trudged along the winding old road for at least another mile, this time taking turns pushing the clunky old bike. Then the road curved and we headed in the direction of the ocean. We left the bike leaning against a tree, gathered all the pails, scrambled through a thicket full of prickers, and finally came out onto a field that stretched to a cliff that dropped way down to rocks and deep water. The ocean seemed angrier here than at our secret cove, I noticed.

"I don't see any strawberries," I said, scanning the field for long, straight furrows and big, bushy green plants like those I'd picked the other day.

"Scooch down and really *look*," Christopher ordered, doing just that. When I followed him down, I still didn't see any big red berries.

"You have to look hard for these," he instructed, gently pushing aside little green leaves to show me miniature berries, the size and color of the little bright red buttons on my top.

"Oh. Ayuh," I said, hoping he'd notice my new vocabulary word. But I didn't dare glance at him to find out.

We picked.

And picked.

And picked.

It took a *very* long time to half-fill my pan. I was hot, sticky, and sweaty. Mosquitoes were biting my neck, which was burning from the sun. The back of my top was drenched. My legs were all scratched. But I was so glad to be with a real, genuine friend that I wasn't going to complain. Finally, when I couldn't stand it any longer, I asked, "Don't we have enough yet? How long do we have to do this?"

"Until all the pails are full," he said, without stopping. I groaned to myself—I thought. He looked over at me and suggested, "Take one. You'll see why we're workin' so hard."

I did. The juice that squirted into my mouth was sweeter than any strawberry I'd ever tasted before.

"Ayuh," I said.

We stopped halfway through the morning for drinks and snacks, which didn't start to fill the hole in my stomach. Still, if Christopher wasn't complaining, I wouldn't, either.

Finally, when the sun was heading far beyond the place where it should be for lunch, Christopher said we could stop. We surveyed the pans and rearranged the berries, hoping to make the pans look fuller. We scrambled to find a few more berries, and then headed back through the thicket to the bike.

"I'll walk you home," he offered, as he carefully arranged the tin buckets in a row across the old bike's handlebars.

"You can't carry all these to South Portland and back without spilling some. I'll walk you home!"

Once again, he gave me that funny little look before he finally nodded.

* * *

I don't know how long it took us to navigate that old bike around potholes, while balancing the pails so they wouldn't spill, but it seemed to take forever. My arms were ready to drop off, they were so sore from stretching, picking, pulling, and lugging pans and pails. As we slowly made our way down the dirt road, we seemed to be leaving South Portland behind, but I didn't ask any questions. Christopher is one of those kids you'll follow, no matter what you're thinking.

Finally, when I could smell the salt in the air again, he turned the bike onto a narrow, rutted dirt lane that wound through dark evergreens. At the end of the lane, we stepped around a mountain of wooden lobster traps and a small mound of green wire lobster traps, and I saw a shed whose shingles had been bleached by the sun until they were as silver as the belly of a big old codfish. Yellow-and-blue buoys dangled from the walls of the shed, which tilted at an angle. More buoys and barrels were scattered on the ground around it.

"Do you live *there*?" I asked.

Christopher gave me that funny look again and I felt my face grow hot. I wanted to bite my tongue. But he just said, "No, that's Dad's lobster shed. Our house is over there."

Christopher's home looks like a picture I'd seen in my history book when we were studying the Pilgrims in Plymouth Colony. My teacher called it a Cape Cod house. It has a steep, slanted roof, tiny little windows, and a front door made of thick, wide old boards with three little square panes of thick, greenish glass close to the top. Nothing on this house looks like it has ever been painted. Over lots and lots of years, the clapboards had weathered to a dark brown, the color of Papa's piano, and the roof had decided to droop a little in the middle. A jungle of flowers surrounded the house.

When we stepped inside, I could smell something spicy and good, but I couldn't see anything until my eyes adjusted to the cool darkness. Christopher took my hand and led me through a winding, narrow hallway until we came into the kitchen, which faces the ocean. Thanks to the open door and the sunshine sparkling on the water and reflecting through the windows, the kitchen was very bright and sunny.

* * *

"Mum. This is Elizabeth. Betsy, I mean. She helped me pick the berries," Christopher said kind of shyly, prodding me forward with his hand at my back.

The cramped little room seemed to be crawling with people and pets. I recognized Amos, Samuel, Benjamin, Charles, and Rebecca from their occasional appearances at Grammie's house. They were all peeling, stirring, or running to fetch things. A very little boy dressed in a droopy diaper was crawling on a countertop screeching *"Kitty!...Kitteeeee!,"* chasing a kitten who didn't look like she wanted to be caught. In the middle of the room stood a woman whose hair had been pulled into a bun.

The woman's sleeves were rolled up and her forehead was wet. She was working hard to stir whatever was inside a huge yellow bowl set on a battered wooden table. She had a bundle of something on her shoulder. When I looked again, I saw that it was a sleeping baby that she somehow managed to keep balanced while she worked. At her feet slept a brown-and-white dog with a feathery kind of tail, who didn't seem to notice all the noise and activity. Cuddled around the dog's middle were three or four puppies, all equally sleepy.

"How do you do, Mrs. Knight?" I stepped out of the shadows and put my hand out, just like my parents had taught me to do, but there was no way she was able to shake a hand, even if she'd wanted to.

When I got a good look at her, I kind of gasped, I guess. Mrs. Knight looked like an older, woman version of Christopher. She had the same tanned, freckled face, the same reddish-brown hair, and the same way of holding her head on her neck. Kind of proud and shy at the same time. She also had the same bright blue eyes, though hers looked very tired right now, with lines crisscrossing around them. She looked at me with her eyebrows raised a little, not saying anything. At last she smiled. A warm, sweet kind of smile.

I breathed out a breath that I hadn't realized I'd been holding for a long, long time.

Chapter 17

"Betsy!"

"Betsy!"

"Betsy!"

"Betsy!"

"Betsy!"

Amos, Samuel, Benjamin, Charles, and Rebecca squealed as they dropped the things they were working on and ran to me.

"Did you find the treasure?"

"Did you?"

"Did you bring it home?"

"Did you?"

"Did you see any pirates?"

"Is there enough treasure for bikes for *all* of us?"

They asked so many questions and they asked them so loud and so fast that I didn't know where to look first. As they crowded around me, the small room felt like it was shrinking. I wanted to step back and catch a breath, but I was afraid to move. I worried I'd step on someone or something.

This was a *very* different kitchen from the silent, shiny aqua-and-chrome kitchen my parents have in Chicago. Unless we have a party, we never have much going on in our kitchen and I only visit it when I clear the dining room table, get myself a snack, or help Mom make fruitcakes at Christmastime. For sure, our kitchen never heard noise like this. I tried to sort out all the voices and understand what everyone was saying.

"Whoa! Whoa!" Christopher said with a grin. "The treasure we found today was hidden under strawberry leaves. You can eat it, but you can't buy bikes with it."

He led me out the open back door with his brothers and sister trailing behind us and we showed them the pails and pans full of strawberries. "Only one apiece until Mum tells us otherwise," he told his crew.

Each of the heads peered over each bucket, carefully choosing the biggest, reddest, juiciest berry they could find. Then we formed a procession, carrying our morning's work into the kitchen.

"Ayuh. Good enough," Mrs. Knight said, after inspecting our loot. "You must be hungry. Why don't you make yourself some lunch before you pick the strawberries over?"

Pick the strawberries over? Wasn't once enough? I wondered, but the idea of lunch sounded good enough to me that I was willing to do anything afterward.

"May I have a fluffernutter, please?" I asked politely, with visions of a plump sandwich in my hands.

Everyone in that busy little kitchen stopped what they were doing and stared at me. My face turned real hot.

"A what?" Mrs. Knight finally broke the silence.

"A peanut butter and Marshmallow Fluff sandwich?" I asked meekly.

Christopher said quickly, "Mum, Betsy is from Chicago and they do things a little differently there."

"We don't have peanut butter here," Amos said. "We only have bread and butter and sometimes cinnamon sugar to sprinkle on it."

Christopher didn't say anything as he quickly spread butter on bread and, with a nod from his mother, sprinkled the tiniest dusting of sugar across the top. I felt like sinking under the floorboards while he worked and the kids stared at me.

We ate outside under a tree looking over the ocean, with the gang of little brothers, sister, kittens, and puppies coming and going around us. For awhile we didn't say anything. I was wondering why a family living in 1957 wouldn't know what a fluffernutter was and Christopher was probably wondering why he'd brought me home.

"He's never done that before, you know," Rebecca whispered to me. "We don't have other kids here very often."

At last, just when I was beginning to feel really hot and embarrassed, two seagulls started hovering over our heads, squawking at us and dive-bombing nearby. The regular, comfortable feeling between Christopher and me began to come back. When we started laughing at the birds, we were almost back to normal.

Christopher had his brothers carry the pails to us under the trees and he showed me how to pick the berries over, pulling off the green tops and looking for teeny, tiny bugs and little sticks and leaves. Every once in awhile, a little brown hand would appear between us and snatch a berry out from under our hands. It became a game to keep the pails upright and full enough for jam-making. Trying to keep his next-to-smallest brother entertained, Christopher made up a story about how seagulls are the spies for pirates. Everyone waited until he had finished his story before they wandered back into the kitchen to their interrupted chores. By the time Chris and I finished with the strawberries, our hands—and little Sam's mouth—were bright red.

* * *

"It's Howdy Doody time!" I announced with a big smile as we returned to the kitchen carrying big dishpans full of clean berries.

Once again, they all stopped what they were doing. Once again, the noisy room went quiet and everyone stared at me.

"What's Howdy Doody time?" Rebecca finally asked.

"You know! The television show! How everything starts when Captain Bob says, 'It's Howdy Doody time?'" I answered, feeling kind of weak around my stomach. "That's what my parents and I always say when we're about to start something."

More silence. Then, "We don't have a television," Amos said.

"Oh," I said.

But I found it hard to believe them. Why wouldn't they have a television set? I couldn't imagine what life would be like without watching *Bonanza* at 7:30 on Saturday nights. Or *The Lawrence Welk Show* with my grandparents. And I liked to watch goofy old Theodore get into trouble on the *Leave It To Beaver Show.* But I wasn't about to ask any more questions or say any other odd thing in this kitchen, I decided.

Good thing, too, I guessed, when I snuck a glance at Christopher's face.

* * *

Well, the afternoon got better. Mrs. Knight let me use the round, silver masher to squish the berries. Then we measured them, poured them into a big, heavy black pot, and started simmering the mixture—"mess," she called it—on the old enamel stove. She carefully measured sugar, grain by grain, until she had just what she needed for the strawberries, plopped in a chunk of butter, and added apple juice. I stirred the pot until the strawberries thickened.

Meanwhile, Christopher had the hard job. After Rebecca washed the jam jars, he put a silver knife in every one, then poured boiling water from a huge teakettle into the jars, trying not to scald his hands or slop water onto the floor—or a baby, kitten, puppy, toy, or dog.

When the mixture was thick enough and very bubbly, Mrs. Knight carried the big kettle to the kitchen sink and skimmed pink sugary foam off the top of the jam. One by one, Christopher picked up each jar and poured out the hot water, carefully keeping the hot knife inside until his mother ladled the jam almost to the top of each jar.

My next job was to melt wax in a little frying pan, making sure it didn't burn. When Christopher's hot water job was done, he took the frying pan and poured a little pool of melted wax onto the top of each jam jar.

"What's that for?" I asked.

"Keeps the jam sterile," his mother explained. "We'll pop the wax off when we open the jar. This batch should last us for half the winter or so. You both did a fine job for me today."

This was the most that I'd heard Christopher's mother say all afternoon and the words made me proud in a way I hadn't ever felt before. I wanted her to like me, so I said, "Ayuh. Shoah." Then I cringed a little when I saw Christopher's face. Did he think I was making fun of her? Oh, how I hoped not!

At the end of a very long day, after the mess was cleaned up, we made another mess, getting our hands and cheeks all sticky when we smeared the frothy foam from the top of the jam onto slabs of bread and gobbled them down. Gee, was that good!

After Christopher and I washed the faces and hands of all his little brothers and sister, he walked me outside and said he'd take me home.

"Why don't you use one of our bikes? We'll get you there quicker," he suggested, leading me to a graveyard of bicycles.

The moment I'd been dreading had arrived.

"I don't know how to ride a bike," I admitted. Once again, my face felt as hot as the late-afternoon sun.

I just knew he'd think I was stupid or ask me why not, but to my relief he didn't.

"Well, maybe we can change that some day. But for now, why don't you climb on my handlebars and I'll ride you home?"

Wow! This was the first time I'd ever been offered a chance to do something my parents considered dangerous. For one moment I hesitated, knowing what they would want me to say, but the offer was too tempting. And, besides, if Christopher did something, it couldn't be dangerous or wrong. He was my lighthouse.

* * *

"Whee!" I shrieked, with the wind flapping my hair into my eyes, as we careened down Shawmut Street. This was the most fun I'd ever had! I flipped my head, trying to clear the hair out of my sight. Then I saw them. The gang of five. Just ahead, leaning against their shiny Schwinns and trading baseball cards. When they heard me squeal, they turned their heads and stared.

"Found yourself a girlfriend, Christopher?" the one called Nick asked.

"Did this witch forget her broom, Chris?" Sam called out.

Christopher eased the bike to a stop and I slid down off the handlebars, scraping my leg on the spokes, wondering what would happen now. I glanced a little fearfully at him, wondering what he'd say.

"Hi, guys."

He looked at them and they looked at him. Then he said, "I should introduce you to Betsy. She came here all the way from Chicago. She's an expert on pirates."

When he started talking, the boys kind of clamped their jaws shut tight, like they didn't care if I was from the moon. But when they heard about the pirates, they seemed to reconsider. I was afraid Christopher would tell them about our hunt for treasure, but he didn't.

"What do you know about pirates?" Nick finally asked. The others looked like they were glad he did.

"I know the names of all the pirate captains who sailed off the coast of Maine. I know that they hid treasure in coves up and down the coast. I know that they killed the shipmates who helped them bury the treasure so no one would be alive to tell about it. And I know that sometimes those dead mates haunt the area where treasure is buried, to keep away treasure hunters," I said, casually, keeping my eye out for a hidden supply of mud. "Well, I've got to be going now. Thanks for the ride, Christopher."

I walked the rest of the way home, hoping that I looked cool and casual instead of scared and lonely.

* * *

"How is the strawberry picker?" Papa asked as soon as I walked into the kitchen. He was hovering close by the cupboard where Grammie was sliding ginger cookies off a cookie sheet.

"Good, but tired," I said, flopping down onto a chair and sticking my feet up on the one next to it. "It takes a lot of berries to make a few jars of jam. And it takes a lot of mosquitoes to pick a lot of berries."

I told them a little about Christopher's family over that night's boiled dinner. (Another New England tradition, a boiled dinner has corned beef, potatoes, onions, parsnips, cabbage, and carrots all cooked together in what my grandmother calls "liquor," but everyone else would call juice.) We talked about the little old house and the big crowd in the kitchen, the cute puppies, noisy little brothers and sister, and the seagulls that shared our lunch.

"Everything was good, but I always say the wrong things," I told my grandparents after a little while. "They didn't know anything I was talking about and they don't have the kinds of things I'm used to."

"Fortunately, we aren't measured by the things we have, Betsy, or by the house we live in, or by the bicycles we ride," Papa said, putting his hand on my shoulder. "There are more important ways to measure people—by what's in their heart and by the things that they say and do."

I didn't know what was in Christopher's heart, but I did know that it was a good one. He always seemed to say and do the right thing.

And I sure didn't.

All that night, I worried that the boys' taunts would keep Christopher away.

Chapter 18

I woke up to the sounds of rain drumming and thumping on the roof of my grandparents' house and the wind roaring around the chimney. As the foghorn howled in the distance, I knew *exactly* how it felt. I could have done a little howling myself! I wanted to go to the beach with my friend—and I wasn't sure if I still had a friend.

Fortunately, just as Grammie pulled muffins from the oven, Christopher arrived, rain dripping from his yellow slicker and rain hat.

After we'd eaten, Papa suggested, "Why don't you ask your grandmother to tell you about the treasure she found on your beach when she was a little girl?"

Christopher and I looked at my grandmother in surprise. She didn't seem like the treasure-hunting sort of person.

"Perhaps the children don't want to hear an old story," she said.

"We do!" we said together.

We both took a heaped-up bowl of strawberries, an extra

muffin or two, and a glass of milk and trooped out onto the front porch, where, under the shelter of the roof, Great-Grammie was rocking and humming that funny little song—except this time I didn't think that it sounded scary at all, just sort of comforting on a rainy day.

"Well, it all began like this…," Grammie said, sipping tea from a china cup.

* * *

"When I was a little girl, winters seemed longer and storms seemed stronger than they do now. One year, 1907, was especially bad. Sudden storms—even hurricanes—would sweep up across the ocean, leaving disaster in their wake. The winds would howl and the rains would slap across our windows. When the storms were over, we'd hear terrible stories of men washed overboard from the decks of big sailing ships. We often read about ships that disappeared, never to be seen or heard from again.

"Several times that autumn, the fire alarm would sound—a long ring, then a short ring, then another long ring, over and over again—announcing trouble at sea. All the men, no matter what they were doing, would race to the beach and climb into boats, if they could, to help rescue people out at sea. They would set up rigs called breech buoys, which were lines with cables strung from shore out to a ship in trouble. One by one, shipwrecked women and children would climb into what looked like a pair of heavy man's pants and they would fly across the water on those cables to safety. The men would come last—if the ship hadn't sunk yet.

"Those were exciting times, but also very scary times. The whole community rejoiced when someone was saved and the whole community mourned when someone was lost."

I looked quickly at Christopher, remembering our conversation about the dangers of the ocean. He was concentrating on my grandmother's words.

"Well, one week the mothers kept all the children home from school because the storms were especially harsh. The winds howled night and day, day and night. Shards of ice pelted our windows and roofs. Trees and signs were broken as easily as you could break a match stick. The foghorn bellowed non-stop for ten long, frightening days. It almost seemed as though the Bible's end times were about to begin."

From the widow's walk, a little room perched on the tippy-top of Grammie's girlhood house on Shawmut Street, my grandmother's family could see far out to sea.

"My uncle Benjamin Henley, an old salt, would pace the deck of that widow's walk through the stormy nights and days with his spyglass trained on the waves, straining his eyes to see a mast—but hoping against hope that the sailors at sea had all known enough to head for safe harbors and ports."

Then, one day, Grammie said, her uncle came thumping down the stairs as fast as he could move, yelling that a four-masted schooner was foundering on the rocks of the island off the shore. Grammie's brothers were sent racing to the firehouse to sound the alarm. Everyone jumped into boots, grabbed slickers and rain hats, and headed for the beach.

The waves were as high as a building and so ferocious that even the bravest and strongest sailors couldn't row hard enough to get a boat off the beach, Grammie said, so the crowd of anxious townspeople watched helplessly on the shore as the ship keeled over and sank.

"We all stood there like statues through the night of November 11, 1907, hoping for a miracle, praying hard, and straining our eyes to see if a lifeboat or a mast would float to shore with someone clinging for safety. But we saw nothing. No one," Grammie said with an unhappy and faraway look in her eyes.

"The weary, saddened neighbors trudged home through the storm and slept fitfully through what was left of the night," she continued. "We awakened the next day as if we had been dreaming. The seas were sparkling blue and nearly glassy. The sky was equally blue. The winds had died away altogether.

"Well, everyone hurried back to the beach, expecting to see debris from the ship that had been so badly battered on the rocks. But there wasn't a board or a barrel to indicate a shipwreck from the night before."

Grammie told us that the newspapers reported a mystery surrounding that ship. Not one four-masted schooner had been sighted along the coast for a month and not one shipping company had reported the loss of such a ship.

A week later, her neighbors found the figurehead from a large ship's prow washed ashore on Willard Beach. It was an unusual carving for a ship; instead of a mermaid or a beautiful lady or a sea monster, it was a little girl smiling and holding a folded umbrella in her hand. Stuck in the sand down the beach was a carved and gilded nameboard, which said *The Fair Weather.*

"Clerks in the Commerce Building set to work to identify the ship and its passengers and owners, but the last ship registered under that name had sailed many years earlier," Grammie told us. "The more they researched, the stranger the story became. That *Fair Weather,* crewed entirely by men and boys from Portland, had sailed around the horn to California, carrying passengers from Maine to the Gold Rush in the West…

"*The Fair Weather* sank in a storm off Portland, Oregon

110

(which was named for our city, you know) on November 11, 1857. No passengers or crew members survived."

I'll bet that Christopher felt as astonished as I did. I quickly did the math: those accidents had been exactly fifty years and a whole country apart. But that wasn't the most amazing part of the story. Grammie kept talking, looking so far into the past that she didn't seem to realize that we were still beside her.

"On the afternoon when the newspaper reported that strange mystery, I went to our special cove next to Willard Beach all by myself. I'm not exactly sure why I did it, but I brought my little gardening shovel and started digging close to the high-water mark. I'd gotten about a foot down in the sand when my shovel hit something that sounded hollow. I dropped to my knees in the wet sand and dug and dug…."

"What was it, Grammie?" we both asked breathlessly.

Then Christopher coughed and said, "I mean, Mrs. Leighton."

"It was a beautiful little chest, with fancy brass trim," she said, and her eyes looked as though they were seeing that chest for the first time.

Somehow, the little girl managed to drag the chest all the way home by herself. By the time her father had returned home and set to work on the lock, the chest and my grandmother were surrounded by a crowd of excited friends and neighbors.

"What was inside?" I felt like I didn't have any breath left as I waited for the answer.

"A beautiful china doll—the one that sits upstairs on my bureau. A baby's christening gown and bonnet; my own baby—your mother—would wear it one day many years later. A ship's logbook with the inscription *The Fair Weather*. An old-fashioned picture called a daguerrotype of a smiling family with one boy and three little girls—that picture is on the bookshelf in our parlor. And this—"

Grammie pulled a chain out from under the neckline of her dress and Christopher and I leaned in to peer at a gold heart-shaped locket. On the back, the name "Esther" was engraved.

"Your name is Esther!" I said excitedly.

Grammie just nodded with a strange look on her face.

"What did the logbook say?" Christopher asked.

"Unfortunately, the book had been soaked and the ink had smeared so that all we could read was the date.

"1857."

Wow! I mean, wow! That was the most amazing story I'd ever heard! Better than anything Nancy Drew had ever told me! I had shivers running up and down my back and prickly feelings on my head. I wouldn't have been surprised if my braids were standing on end. I had a thousand questions and yet I knew that probably not one would ever be answered.

After gasping for a minute or two, I looked at Christopher and he looked at me.

"Grampie always says that the ocean keeps its secrets," he said solemnly.

My Grammie nodded.

I didn't know what he meant. Not then, anyway.

Chapter 19

Christopher and I had to wait impatiently through the weekend before we could head to our secret cove again. That Monday when he arrived shortly after breakfast with the newspaper, he said he could only stay a couple of hours because his father needed him to work on lobster traps. I didn't *dare* offer to help him with that chore. Grammie packed a quick lunch—of fluffernutters. (I didn't want Christopher to think I'd made up this sandwich just to show off when I was visiting his house.)

This time we left Great-Grammie sleeping when we headed to Willard Beach. We scurried up the rocks to our cove and starting digging. No fooling around today. We dug and dug all around the spot where we'd found the giant bottle, hoping for a find like the one my grandmother had discovered there, but the sun was hot and the sand seemed empty.

"Just one more square and we'll have to go," Christopher said. Right afterward, my shovel clunked on what sounded like metal. We got down on our knees and scooped sand with our shovels, then our hands. Sand was flying so fast it dusted our faces and scratched our eyes.

We uncovered a small tin container, round and rusting. When we tried to open it, we found the top was stuck on tight. I pulled out my Swiss Army knife. "It has eleven tools," I told Christopher.

"Let's use them!"

"My mother doesn't let me open it," I said.

He reached out his hand, took the knife, and carefully pried open the biggest blade, which was so shiny that it cast a reflection against the nearby rock. Meanwhile, I shook and rattled the can. "I think it's full of jewels!"

I was so excited that I was shivering all over, just like my dog Ebenweezer does when we get his leash for a walk.

Christopher washed the can a couple of times and pried the knife around the edge over and over again. At last he managed to bend the lid off the can a tiny bit at a time. We clunked heads when we both tried to stick our noses over the top of the metal container to see what was inside.

Christopher carefully poured the contents into my hand and we held our breath, hoping we'd see diamonds, sapphires, emeralds, and rubies fall out. But the rocks looked an awful lot like sea glass.

"Maybe they're jewels in disguise, before they're polished for jewelry," I said when Christopher looked so disappointed. "Let's go show them to Grammie. She has a ring with diamonds on it, so she'll know what these are."

We filled our hole, then charged home, hopeful of good news.

Papa and Grammie poured our treasures onto a clean kitchen towel and looked at each one closely. They even put their glasses on to look better.

"Well, I think you've found a fine collection of…" Papa said as Christopher and I fixed our eyes hopefully on him.

"…seaglass."

When he saw our disappointment, he added, "There are some fine pieces here—red, blue, even amber and unusual shades of purple. Someone worked very hard to gather this collection."

"No bicycles today," Christopher said with a disappointed sigh, as he headed for his sister's old purple bike and an afternoon working on lobster traps.

"Can you come back tomorrow, Christopher?" I yelled before he disappeared around the corner.

He turned to look at me and shaded his eyes against the sun.

"Ayuh," he yelled and waved before he headed home.

Chapter 20

"This is going to be one of those rare and perfect days that prove without a doubt that Maine is the finest place in the world," Papa said early the next morning.

Standing beside my grandfather on the back porch, I watched a huge round orange ball rise over the horizon, reflecting the colors of the marigolds in Grammie's flower garden. I didn't need any convincing. I had a feeling that something special was going to happen today and I didn't want to waste any time getting to it. I stood silently beside Papa for long minutes, enjoying the butterflies-in-my-stomach feeling and the warm breeze that promised a happy day.

If I was up early, Great-Grammie Henley was up even earlier. She was sitting at the kitchen table nibbling blueberry muffins and staring out the window, and she had dressed herself today, I could tell. Her housedress was on backward, thick winter stockings were rolled below her knees, her floppy slippers were on the wrong feet, and she was wearing the new hat Grammie had given her for Mother's Day. Next to her plate sat a pair of white gloves and her purse (empty except for a dime, a clean handkerchief, and a slip of paper with her name, my grandparents' names, address, and telephone number on it).

"Good morning, my dear!" Grammie called cheerfully as the kitchen door creaked behind her. Her arms were full of flowers in a rainbow of colors. "A very happy birthday to you!"

"Grammie! You remembered!" I hadn't really doubted it, but I was still glad to know it.

"Of course we did! Your birth was one of our red letter days," Papa added as he followed Grammie into the kitchen.

And speaking of letters, according to my last letter from Mom and Daddy, their excavation site was seven hours away from Maine in time, so I had leaped out of bed early, hoping to get an early morning phone call...though I'd die rather than tell anyone how much that call would mean to me. So far, no call had come and I was trying not to look as though I was anxiously watching the clock and the telephone.

"My birthday!" Great-Grammie interrupted.

Did she always have to claim everything that was mine?

But, evidently, this time she did, because Grammie hugged her, too, and said, "Yes, Edna. Today is your special day, too!"

"Really, Grammie? This couldn't be her *exact* birthday, is it?" I asked.

"It is, indeed," she said. "You were born eleven years ago, in 1946, and she was born eighty-two years before that, in 1864. You were born far to the west in Chicago—I was there for that special day—and Mama was born far away Down East on Deer Isle in the midst of the Civil War."

Every day on my way to Ralph Waldo Emerson Elementary School, I walked past the hospital where I was born, but

118

Deer Isle has never had a hospital. Great-Grammie had been born in the old Knowlton farmhouse at Sunset, overlooking the ocean, my grandmother told me. Great-Grammie's father had been the little boy who'd been shipwrecked; after that, he became a farmer. Her mother, whose name was Sarah Ann Small before she married, lived up to her maiden name, Grammie told me.

"She was actually very small as a grown woman—four feet, ten inches," Grammie continued. "Mama wasn't a lot bigger than that. She was the second of eight children."

"I only know about Steve, Edna, and Erolyn. Who were the others?"

"Except for her youngest sister, Elizabeth, they all died as babies or very small children," Grammie said. I looked quickly at the doll Great-Grammie was holding. She called her Elizabeth! I opened my mouth to ask more questions, but Grammie hurriedly changed the subject by asking, "And what would our birthday girl like to do today? I think that I can guarantee that whatever it is, we'll all be happy to oblige."

With Papa's help, we discussed all the options, from the impossible ("A trip to the moon?"; "A day at Disneyland?") to the possible ("A picnic at Two Lights?"; "A shopping trip to the stores on Congress Street?"; "A tour of Longfellow's house?"). We finally decided on a picnic at the Eastern Promenade in Portland with my favorite food: Italian sandwiches from Amato's ("extra pickles, no onions, please"), the peppery-tasting soda called Moxie, and maraschino cherry cake. We could eat while we listened to the Thursday night band concert, Grammie said.

"Could Christopher come, too?" I asked.

"I can't think of a better dinner guest," she said.

"Do you think Great-Grammie would mind if we helped her change her clothes before we went?" I asked a little timidly.

"That can be arranged."

* * *

"Happy birthday, Elizabeth-called-Betsy!"

Christopher knocked on the screen door and came into the kitchen with his hands held behind his back.

"How did you know?" I tried not to look as happy as I felt.

"You told me the first day we met that you'd be eleven on the eleventh and I asked your Grammie which month," he admitted kind of shyly. After a pause, he said, "I have two presents for you."

The first present he pulled out from behind his back. It was the craziest package I'd ever seen, a queer shape with odd angles wrapped in what looked like a brown paper bag with a pink bow stuck on top.

I couldn't imagine what it was and I couldn't wait to open it. I didn't carefully pry the paper open in the ladylike way my mother was always suggesting. I ripped it from stem to stern, as Papa would say. What I saw made my mouth drop open.

It was a miniature white lighthouse attached so cunningly to a piece of silvery driftwood that when it was set down on the table, it looked like a faraway lighthouse perched on a granite cliff. There were even little carved evergreen trees surrounding the lighthouse. A cord dangled from the back.

I kind of gasped. Not just because it was the first present a friend had ever given me without an invitation to a birthday party. Not just because I was surprised and loved it. It was because I wondered if Christopher somehow knew that I thought of him as a lighthouse-kind-of-person.

I was speechless. For once.

"It lights up," he said, not waiting for me to thank him. He plugged the cord into an electric socket on Grammie's counter and a tiny lightbulb brightened the top of the lighthouse.

"I couldn't figure out how to make the light blink, so you'll just have to imagine that it does," he said, finally looking up at me. His smile faded when he saw the tears in my eyes.

"Don't you like it?" he asked anxiously.

"Christopher, it's wonderful!" I hugged him hard, then realized that I'd just hugged a boy. I stepped back real quick, putting my hands behind my back. My face felt like it was painted bright red.

"Don't worry, son. Tears are part of the mystery of women. If you live to be twice my age, you'll never figure them out," Papa said, trying to make Christopher feel better, I guess.

Christopher told us that his grandfather had been teaching him how to carve. "My father helped me with the wiring, so it's safe. Amos and Rebecca helped me paint it. They wanted you to know," he added.

"I'll think of you all every time I look at it," I promised, feeling shy for some reason. Christopher looked me in the eyes for a long time before he nodded. Then, "Oh! I almost forgot. Your second present is out by the shed."

Grammie, Papa, and I followed Christopher out into the yard, with Great-Grammie trailing behind us. I saw not only one rickety old bicycle, but two, leaning on the shed. I looked around for its owner while trying to spot another brown paper package.

"I'm going to teach you how to ride a bicycle today!" Christopher announced.

Suddenly my knees felt shaky. My mouth felt dry. My stomach felt sick.

Chapter 21

My worst nightmare was about to come true.

"Gee...thanks, Christopher. But I don't think I can ride a bicycle this summer," I said in a little voice, trying to avoid the eyes looking at me.

"Sure you can, Betsy! You'll learn fast," Christopher promised.

Oh, why did this moment have to come now? Why did it have to ruin a perfectly fine birthday?

Three years ago for my birthday, my parents had given me a beautiful, shiny-new pink Schwinn with a pink flowered basket and my own personal license plate on the back. Miss Noyes, my nanny, had wheeled it to the park and kept pushing me from the back fender. I'd wobbled and wandered from ditch to ditch, smashing into signs and crashing into bushes, falling again and again and again. I wouldn't let her see that I was crying inside. The scrapes on my knees and arms didn't throb half as much as the hurts on my heart. She kept hollering in her loud voice, "Children much younger than you know how to ride a bicycle! What's the matter with you?" I'd wheeled my new bike, by then dusty and banged-up, home in disgrace. Several days later it disappeared from our apartment garage. No one ever mentioned it again.

Now I had to face my worst memories.

"I don't think my parents would like me to ride a bike," I said.

"They'll be pleased to know that you learned," Papa said.

"Kids in Chicago can't ride bikes because there's too much traffic," I said.

"There are parks," Grammie said.

"That bike looks too big for me," I said.

"Christopher and I can lower the seat," Papa said.

My knees started wobbling and knocking, and my mouth felt like it was full of dry cotton balls. My stomach felt even worse.

"I don't think I'll be very good at riding." I tried to avoid Christopher's eyes.

"Everybody has to start some time. What a fine way to remember your eleventh birthday!" I guess Papa thought he was being encouraging.

Suddenly Christopher spoke up very quietly. "You don't have to if you don't want to, Betsy."

I didn't have a lot of experience with best friends, but I could tell that his feelings were hurt. I had to decide fast. Would I rather lose my new best friend because he would find out I was a loser? Or would I rather lose my new best friend because I refused to accept his present?

I decided I'd risk being seen as a loser.

"No, if you think I can, then I want to," I said with a scaredy-cat little voice. I walked over to the bike. "I just hope this is over quick," I whispered to myself.

But, to my surprise, I didn't fall a gazillion times. My nanny had just shoved me from behind, then stood where she was to watch me fall. Christopher ran with me, keeping one hand on my shoulder and the other on the back of the seat. Gradually he took his hand off my shoulder and, before I knew it, his hand was off the back of the seat, too.

"I did it! I can ride!" I shouted. My smile stretched across my whole face, I was so happy. The wind whistled past my cheeks and my hair flopped excitedly around my face as I took off down the Shawmut Street hill just a little wobbly, leaving Christopher and my grandparents far behind.

"Use the brakes, Betsy!" Christopher yelled as Mr. Sullivan's old black car came squealing around the corner just ahead of me.

Christopher dashed up in time to fish me out of Mrs. Turner's rose bushes, where I'd landed head-first.

"Is the bike hurt?" I asked, anxiously.

"Nope. Neither are the roses. Let's go back up the hill to get my bike."

Suddenly, to my eyes, that rusting, battered, bruised old bike looked beautiful. It made me feel free in a way I'd never felt before. For the rest of the morning, we toured South Portland on wheels. We rode through Fort Preble, waving at the soldiers we passed. We wandered along the back roads leading to the strawberry fields and marshes. We explored the playgrounds of all the schools in town, including the George F. Henley School, which is where Christopher and his brothers and sisters had all gone to primary classes.

"I asked Mrs. Leighton and she told me that this school is named for her grandfather, who was the school superintendent. That's your great-great-grandfather," Christopher told me. "My parents and my Grampie went to school there."

Wow! I hadn't known anything about that Henley! When you hear something like that, it makes you feel glad that you got good grades on your report card!

We stopped long enough for peanut-butter-and-banana sandwiches and went home. I tried to be casual when I asked my grandparents a couple of times if the phone had rung that day, but Grammie just said that Great-Aunt Elizabeth had called and would be coming to dinner with us. Christopher looked at me every time I asked that question, but I don't think he knew why I wondered.

I hung around a little longer, listening for Grammie's special *Ring! Ring!...Ring!...Ring!* It didn't come, so we headed back to Willard Beach, lugging two shovels as we rode. It didn't seem like any old pirate wanted to give me a special birthday present that day. We didn't find anything but a collection of clamshells.

"I guess we can't find treasures every day. That would make it too easy, Christopher," I said when I saw his disappointment. "Besides, who needs a new bike when this one takes you where you want to go, anyway?"

He looked the way I felt when I was listening for the phone call that didn't come. He shrugged and smiled a little wobbly smile and left me at Shawmut Street so he could deliver the afternoon papers.

Chapter 22

"So this is the young man who has taught our Betsy to ride a bicycle!" Great-Aunt Elizabeth smiled at Christopher after he finished his paper route and parked his bike by our garden shed. She reached out her hand and he shook it with a return smile.

This great-aunt is one of my favoritest people in the world. Tiny and white-haired, her eyes twinkle just like my grandmother's do. She never had kids of her own, so she's a friend to every kid. She's kind of an old version of a girl, actually. She likes all the same things I do: pineapple-orange ice cream, cream-filled doughnuts, barbecue potato chips, Nancy Drew books, picnics, play-acting, and puppies. She seems kind of glamorous for an old lady because she always wears high heels and pretty clothes (no housedresses for her), and she drives a fancy dark green Cadillac.

Grammie never learned to drive, so if she wanted to go anywhere by car, she went with her sister or with Papa. "She was always too busy looking at the people and places she was passing instead of the road," Papa always explains with a smile in his eyes when he looks at his wife. "The trash cans and mail boxes took too much of a beating."

I showed my great-aunt Chris's present. After she marveled at the lighthouse with the light that really works, she gave me my birthday present—a red-haired, pony-tailed doll dressed in a frilly pink-and-white striped dress with matching socks and white leather shoes with tiny rosebuds.

"Gee! Thanks! I love her!" I gave Great-Aunt Elizabeth a big hug.

Christopher looked a little disgusted when he saw my present. I could hear Papa whisper to him, "That's another female thing we don't have to understand."

* * *

"Mama! Happy birthday to you, too!" Great-Aunt Elizabeth said, handing her a big box wrapped in beautiful flowered paper.

Great-Grammie didn't even look at her daughter. She dropped the present on the grass unopened, bent over, and pulled the fancy ribbon off the box, and wrapped it around her doll's head, tying it into a bow. Great-Aunt Elizabeth sighed and turned to Grammie.

"How has she been today? Does she even know that it's her birthday?"

"She knows. And she knows that it's Betsy's birthday, too. Someday she'll remember you, you know," Grammie said consolingly as the two old ladies looked at their mother playing with her doll. Great-Aunt Elizabeth just sighed again.

We packed up blankets, a tablecloth, folding chairs, drinks, and the food, then climbed into Papa's Studebaker. After a stop at Amato's for our sandwiches, we headed to the Eastern Prom (short for Promenade, a funny name for a park), overlooking the Casco Bay at the tippy-top of Portland.

There's a lot to do at this park. The mast from the *U.S.S. Maine* was raised here after the ship was sunk in some long-ago war and the story is told in a monument. There's a sign that tells about the exciting battle between the American ship *Enterprise* and the British ship *Boxer* during the War of 1812—I was glad to see that the Americans won! There's a fancy bandstand where men and women were unpacking shiny instruments and setting up music stands. There's a steep hill for rolling. And there's the harbor, full of sailboats and oil tankers and islands and ancient forts with interesting stories that Papa loves to tell.

But those aren't the stories I remember from this birthday.

After my grandfather had settled Great-Grammie on a folding chair, she saw the sailboats and she clapped her hands. "The Reach! The Reach! We're going across the Reach on my birthday!" She jumped up with her doll in her arms, grabbed my hand, and looked around at Christopher. "Steve! It's time to go! The boat is leaving without us," she called, pulling me fast down toward the water. Her grip on my hand was as hard as my bicycle handle. I was so surprised that I just kept moving beside her without thinking.

"Mama, what on earth—?" Great-Aunt Elizabeth started to exclaim.

"Edna! This is Portland, where Frederick is! Not Deer Isle!" Grammie called out. Christopher dashed down to us, grabbed Great-Grammie's hand, and stopped us just before we would have tumbled down the hill.

It took all five of us to talk my great-grandmother back into her seat and, when we did, she put her knobby old hands over her face and cried and cried. We all felt terrible, especially since this was her birthday. I kind of paced the area around our picnic blanket, feeling embarrassed that other people were watching us. Christopher sat by Great-Grammie's side and patted her arm. Grammie sat on the other side with her arm around her mother's shoulder. She was kind of cooing to her and smoothing her hair, like a mother would do to a baby.

"It's not your time yet, Mama. It's not your time yet. Bye 'n' bye, we'll know when it is," she said over and over again.

Finally, Great-Grammie looked up at her daughter with tears running down the rivers in her cheeks and said, "Mama! Steve and Erolyn are here at last! They need me! I have to go."

All this talk gave me shivers down my spine and I could tell it really shook Great-Aunt Elizabeth up. Her tears fogged up her glasses. Papa cleared his throat and suggested that Christopher walk with him to the car to get more chairs and blankets, in case the night got cooler. Christopher went, but he turned his head and looked back at us as they walked away.

* * *

"What's so special about Great-Grammie's island that she always wants to go there?" I asked when we finally started eating our sandwiches and the band members started squeaking and squawking their instruments as they tuned up for the concert.

None of the grown-ups said anything at first, and Christopher looked from face to face as we waited for some kind of answer.

Finally, Papa cleared his throat. "Many years ago during the war, when I was in the Navy sailing in faraway waters, I dreamed of Maine every night. Maine represented a place that was peaceful and free and clean and beautiful, even in the

130

midst of a terrible war. But most of all, Maine was home and I was homesick. Every man I knew in those days dreamed of his home, whether it was in the cornfields of Iowa, the mountains of Colorado, the skyscrapers of New York, or the Kansas prairies. Like we used to, Edna dreams of the home she knew as a child."

Great-Aunt Elizabeth started to cry again softly, wiping her eyes with a fancy white handkerchief.

Then Christopher suddenly said, "Betsy, I think it's the same as the way people here feel about the ocean. It's in our blood and we can't help but feel pulled to it."

I looked at that boy hard. If he said it, it had to be true. But the thought was scary to me.

"What was her home like?" I asked.

My grandmother described an ancient white farmhouse with two porches, low ceilings, windows with tiny panes of glass, big fireplaces in every room, creaky old floors, and rope beds where generations of babies had been born and old people had died. Flowering plants tangled in a big garden outside the side porch off the kitchen. An outhouse, empty chicken coop, and barn stand somewhere nearby, she said. I could just picture it in my mind.

"This farm serves the same purpose as our family Bible. When you open it up, it tells the stories of all the people who came before us," Grammie continued.

"The very best part of the farm is its setting, don't you think?" Great-Aunt Elizabeth said. "It stands on a knoll in a field full of old fruit trees, lupine, and daisies. The field crosses a tiny dirt road and rolls on to the sea."

"God himself would choose that spot if He only had one home," Papa added. "No other setting in the world can compare. The sunsets are breathtaking and the ocean sings generations of Knowltons to sleep every night."

"Who lives there now?"

"The house usually stands empty, waiting for family members or friends who need it," Great-Aunt Elizabeth said. "For many years, we kept it unlocked and ready for anyone who wanted shelter and a place away from the busy world. Now we lock it, but everyone on the island knows that the key hangs from a nail under the first step leading up onto the side porch. We keep the place stocked with cans of food, matches, kerosene lanterns, flashlights, and a woodpile, so it's always ready for us."

"When was the last time you were there?" Christopher asked.

"Too long ago," my grandmother sighed. "Nowadays we seem to go only for the funerals of my cousins. Mama is the last Knowlton in her generation and only one of my first cousins on the island is still alive."

"Then let's all go and take Great-Grammie there!" I yelled suddenly. I was so excited about the idea that people at nearby picnics turned around and looked at me. I wondered why no one else had thought of it before.

My suggestion fell over our picnic like a water balloon. Everyone sort of jumped, but no one said anything. Grammie swallowed hard and Great-Aunt Elizabeth started tearing up again.

"Betsy, we just don't think it would be the right thing to do for your great-grandmother now," Papa said. "We've discussed the idea and we think it's best that we keep Edna here."

"But…!"

"Let's talk about something else," Grammie said.

I'd never heard my grandmother speak so strongly before.

* * *

When I think back on my eleventh birthday, I have a jumble of feelings in my stomach and in my memory. I learned to ride a bike and I tasted freedom for the first time in my life. I was loved by some very special people. I got to celebrate my birthday with my first-ever best friend, eating my favorite dinner in my favorite park. I opened the coolest present I'd ever received and I knew right away that it would become my most special treasure.

But, still, I can't help thinking of Great-Grammie crying into her twisted, bumpy old hands as she longed for home. I knew exactly how she felt. My home was halfway across the country. My parents were halfway around the world.

And that darn old telephone never did ring that day. Or the next.

Chapter 23

"Betsy, do you think that we might have gotten the beach wrong? That maybe this isn't the pirates' cove?" Christopher asked as we trudged to our special beach, hauling the red wagon full of our shovels, sifters, sacks, notebooks, pens, and lunch.

"Let's study the pirate book again when we get there and see if we can find any clues in it," I suggested, reminding him, "you know, Grammie found her treasure there and we've already found the pirates' rum bottle. I'm sure the chest must be somewhere nearby. We just have to dig some more."

I wanted more than anything to find pieces of eight and Spanish gold doubloons in our special hidden cove. Not because I had any use for them. I just knew how much Christopher—and his brothers and sister—were counting on us digging up treasure this summer. And the summer was hurrying past.

This time when we passed Mr. Macomb's garden, he was out there spraying his fruit trees inch by inch, looking as much like a grouchy scarecrow as any old man I ever saw. A big, black, snarly dog was sniffing the ground near his feet. He glared at us as we went past and as soon as we were out of earshot I warned Christopher about what Grammie had told me about this man loving his plants and trees more than people.

"He scares me more than my Great-Grammie used to," I whispered to my friend. "He probably eats kids for dinner on dark and stormy nights!"

"Don't let him frighten you," Christopher said. Then he looked at me. "You're a lot braver than you think you are, Betsy."

I was flattered that he thought so—but I knew he was wrong.

We quickly forgot about anything except treasure hunting. After we carried our supplies up and down the granite cliff and hid the wagon, we set to work. We ignored the seagulls and the sparkling waters and whatever might be sailing off the shore. We were in a hurry to find the secrets the sand held for us today.

"My brothers and sister sure would like new bikes," Christopher grunted, as he shoveled sand from one end of our string grid. He didn't need to tell me that. I knew it—and I wanted them to have new bikes, too. I shoveled as hard as I could from the opposite end of the grid.

The day was a scorcher; the heat danced on the sand while we worked. Halfway through the morning, I desperately wanted to stop and splash in the cool waves, but I didn't dare suggest it. Christopher's shovel had gotten a lot deeper than mine had.

"Found something!" he shouted when it was close to lunchtime. He began digging even faster. Sand was flying in all directions and he climbed down into his hole. I knelt by the side of the hole and was quickly covered with flying salt and sand, but I didn't care. Our shovels kept hitting something with a THUD! It sounded like wood...it must be the top of a treasure chest!!!

"We've got something here!" he yelled.

A flat wooden plank came into view. We threw aside our shovels, grabbed Grammie's gardening trowels, and stretched out on our bellies, digging around the wood.

"There's writing on it!" I jumped up and down beside the hole, laughing and dancing. Christopher just clamped his jaw shut and kept working.

It took a very long time to dig the thing out of the sand, but we didn't stop for lunch or drinks. Eventually we realized that it wasn't the cover of a chest. It was a very wide, very old and thick board, carved around the edges and very heavy. It must have soaked in a lot of seawater over the years it lay buried. When we finally managed to pry it out of the hole, we turned the board over, stood it up on the beach, and started brushing the sand away from the writing.

"Maybe it's a signboard, giving a map to the treasure!" I suggested.

"Maybe it's a pirate captain's warning not to disturb the treasure," Christopher added.

But what it was really surprised us.

It was a grave marker.

* * *

"Gosh, Christopher," I whispered. I felt like my eyes were popping out of my head.

A skull and crossbones had been carved into the top of the plank, just like the ones I had seen on the old slate stones on Meetinghouse Hill. We could make out the words "Wiltshire, Engl'd" and "Falmouth, Mass."

"Portland used to be called Falmouth in the old days," Christopher told me after reading the old-fashioned script.

I already knew that Maine was once a part of Massachusetts. We could also read the date 1757. But the name had been worn away by time. We could just make out a faint *E* and a *K*.

"Do you think this beach was a graveyard and it's haunted? Maybe a pirate is buried here!" Even though the sun was shining brightly, I couldn't help shivering.

"Maybe this marker washed away from a graveyard by the sea or on an island," Christopher suggested.

"What do we do with it?"

He thought for a long time, but didn't come up with an idea. "Maybe your grandparents can tell us what to do," he suggested at last.

That board was heavy and hard to push up and over the granite cliff, but we somehow managed. We loaded it onto our wagon, where it hung out over all the sides, and we struggled to push and pull the wagon across the beach. The wheels kept sinking deep into the sand. Once we finally reached the nearest sidewalk, we went back for our shovels and other supplies.

It was a silent walk home. I guessed that Christopher was buried as deep in his thoughts as I was in mine.

Until we reached Mr. Macomb's house, that is.

I should have had a clue that something was up when I saw the row of shiny Schwinns leaning against the big old trees lining the sidewalk, but I was surprised to see five pairs of Keds perched on branches in old Mr. Macomb's apple and cherry trees.

"What are you *doing* up there?" I whispered furiously to the nearest pair of sneakers. "He'll kill you and eat you for dinner!"

I was amazed (and secretly impressed) that anyone was brave enough—or stupid enough—to climb that cranky old man's trees.

A white and scared face peeked at me through the leaves.

"He's on the other side of the yard and he's got a big, ugly looking dog," the voice whispered back.

At that moment, Mr. Macomb and his dog began heading our way. The eyes that peeked at me past baby apples were as big and round and white as a doorknob.

"We're gonna be dead meat," the boy groaned.

Speaking of meat gave me an idea. I grabbed two bologna sandwiches from the basket in our wagon, then ran as far away from the trees in the yard as I could, holding a sandwich out to the dog and whistling. (I'm a good whistler. My dad taught me how to whistle between my teeth.)

Well, the dog's ears perked up when he saw the treat, and he came bounding over to me. I'm not especially brave around big, black, snarly, drooly dogs, but I held my trembling hand out to the dog and frantically waved at Christopher with the other one. He gestured to the boys to back up and climb onto the roof of the nearby garden shed while the dog gulped the sandwich.

"You don't mind if I give your dog a snack, do you, Mr. Macomb?" I asked in my Sunday-go-to-church voice.

He grunted. But he came a little closer to me.

"What's your dog's name?" I tried again, to keep his eyes away from his trees a little longer.

"Cannibal," he said, growling just like the dog had.

My braids seemed to stand on end—they were doing a lot of that this summer. The old man must have seen the shock on my face. Suddenly, something that might have been a smile on someone else's face cracked across his mouth.

"Actually, the name is Arnold," he said.

He looked at me and I looked back at him—but out of the corner of my eye, I could see Christopher helping a pair of sneakers shimmy down the rickety old shed's drain pipe behind the old man's back. I reached down to scratch the dog behind his ears, now that I knew that his name wasn't really Cannibal.

Then Mr. Macomb said something that really surprised me. "You have the looks of your grandmother sixty-some years ago."

"Gee! Do you think so?" I was flattered.

"She was the prettiest girl in the Henley School," he said, then cleared his throat and looked as if he was sorry he'd said it. "She was also chockablock full of mischief, always getting herself and everybody else into scrapes—her, the granddaughter of the superintendent of South Portland schools!"

Really? My Grammie? Getting into trouble? That's something grandparents never bother to tell granddaughters!

"What kind of scrapes did she get into?"

By that time, I'd forgotten all about Christopher, the wagon, the grave marker, and those five pesky boys.

He snorted. "What didn't she do? She once dared a gang of us boys to lead Turners' cow up the stairs of the church belfry. The thing about cows is this: they'll go up stairs with a little coaxing, but they won't come down. We learned that the hard way! When the sexton arrived at the church on Sunday morning, he was some fried. There was the cow mooing for all she was worth, so fiercely that ships at sea could hear her, and the Methodist Mission Board was due to come for their annual visit to the Congregationalists within the hour. Fire departments from miles around had to be called to help us get that blamed cow down. Services had to be canceled for the first time since the Indian wars two hundred and sixty-eight years earlier. The lot of us boys couldn't sit down for a week, we got such a tanning. I've been a Baptist ever since—and it's all your grandmother's fault!"

Apparently, that was just the start of many stories.

"That's not the worst thing your grandmother did," Mr. Macomb added in a growly voice.

"Why, what else did she do?"

"You ask her—I don't tell tales out of school," Mr. Macomb snarled. But, I *think* he winked at me right afterward. (Later, I got the joke: out of school. Get it?)

Wow! My life seemed boring and adventureless after that story. Little white-haired old ladies sure can be full of surprises!

All at once, the old man seemed to decide he'd been friendly enough for one day. "Well, get along with you, now, girl. You're interferin' with my gardenin'."

I turned around to see what Christopher was doing and where the other boys were. Chris was reloading our supplies onto the wagon. He was the only boy in sight.

The old man had also turned to look. He jerked his head in Christopher's direction. "That the Knight boy?"

"Yup."

"Humph! Have him ask his grandfather about the outhouse incident. Your grandmother was in on that, too."

He stared at me and seemed to think about his words carefully before he said slowly, "Sometimes the people you meet when you're very young are the ones you wish you'd held onto when you're very old."

Then he stomped off to the garden shed that had just served as a ladder for five pesky boys.

I was left with my mouth hanging wide open.

* * *

"Christopher, listen to this!" I began, but my friend cut me off.

"Betsy, you were brilliant! And you said you weren't brave! Nancy Drew couldn't have handled that man and dog any better. I never thought those guys would get out of the trees in one piece. When you started talking, they moved faster than I've ever seen anybody move."

I was flattered, but quickly pointed out, "Yeah, but look at how much they appreciated it. They didn't even stick around for a thank you."

"That doesn't matter. Quick thinking and good deeds—those are the things that matter. The guys are grateful," Christopher said, hurrying to catch up with me as I marched down the street and he struggled to pull at the wagon and keep everything from sliding off.

Doggone it! That boy was always right! The five hooligans were hanging around at the next corner, waiting for us. They slowly walked toward us. This time, they didn't look so scary.

"Thanks, Betsy," the red-headed one with the Red Sox hat said hesitantly when I got near enough.

The tallest kid, the one with big teeth, walked up to me holding out his hand. "You saved our lives!"

That was the first time I'd ever shaken hands with a kid before.

"If there's anything we can ever do for you, just let us know," the boy called Nick said, in a voice that kind of croaked, before he shook my hand. The others silently pumped my hand.

I didn't know what to say other than "Sure."

Neither did they. After staring at each other and me for a minute, they climbed onto their bikes and slowly peddled away.

Christopher looked at me and I didn't want to look at him, but I did. He winked.

Darn it! Why couldn't *I* ever be right?

Then I remembered what I'd been trying to tell my friend. "You're not going to believe what I just heard about my grandmother!"

I told him about the cow in the church belfry and he laughed so hard that he dropped the wagon handle and bent right over, holding his stomach. I laughed too when I imagined the look on that old sexton's face when he heard a cow mooing at the top of the church belfry on Sunday morning when special visitors were coming to church.

"I wish I'd known your grandmother when she was a girl," he said with a grin when he could stand straight up again.

"Your grandfather did—Mr. Macomb told me to have you ask him about outhouses!"

Christopher nodded. "I'll go over there on my way home from deliverin' papers—unless your grandmother would rather tell us."

The only thing I didn't tell Christopher—the first personal thing I hadn't told him since I'd met him—was Mr. Macomb's advice about holding onto people. I sure did want to hold onto him as a best friend, though.

I skipped along beside him as we pulled the squeaky old wagon.

Chapter 24

"Grammie—"

"Mrs. Leighton—"

"What's the story about you and outhouses when you were a girl?"

Christopher and I had raced each other the last block home, trying to be the first to find my grandmother. We both shouted the question at the same time, as we rounded the corner of the garden shed. My grandmother was so startled that she dropped the pan of new peas she'd been collecting out in the garden and stared at us.

"Heavens to Betsy! Whoever on this earth told you about that old story?"

"Mr. Macomb!"

"*Ernest* Macomb?"

"Sure!"

"He *spoke* to you?" My grandmother again looked startled. "I haven't had anything but a curt 'Hello' from him in sixty years!"

I started to tell her about what he said about hanging on to people you knew when you're young, but for some reason, I decided I'd better do it when we were alone, after I thought about it a little more.

"He said that we should ask Christopher's grandfather about it, but we thought you could tell us instead!"

Grammie did something I'd never seen anyone do before. She sat right down, plunk, onto one of the metal garden chairs and started to laugh. Except it looked a lot more like crying. She laughed and cried and laughed and cried and laughed as tears ran down her cheeks and she mopped at them with her handkerchief. And then she laughed some more.

Christopher and I looked at each other and shook our heads with hopeful smiles, waiting for her to stop and tell us what was so funny.

At long last, she wiped her eyes and looked up at us.

"I think you'd better ask Bertram Knight," was all she'd say.

"Grammie!"

"Mrs. Leighton!"

"I may not remember the story just the way he would," she continued with a wide smile. "And I wouldn't want to get any of the facts wrong. It's been a long time."

Well, no matter how hard we tried to get her to change her mind, she wouldn't budge, although she would giggle every time we asked.

Finally, to change the subject, she asked, "How was your adventure on the beach?"

That's when Christopher and I remembered that we'd dropped the handle of the wagon a block away from home for our race. "Just a minute! We have something to show you!" we shouted, running back for our find.

By the time we wheeled the wagon into the driveway, Papa and Grammie were waiting with lemonade and molasses hermits.

"Will you look at that?" Papa marveled as he inspected the old grave marker. "This is an antique if I ever saw one."

"E. K.," Grammie whispered, running her fingers back and forth across the marker, probably hoping that some other letters would pop off the board.

"Seventeen fifty-seven. Exactly two hundred years ago," Papa pointed out. "And a skilled craftsman did this carving. What a find!"

We suggested touring all the islands offshore, looking for old cemeteries so we could return it (and maybe look for pirate treasure along the way).

Papa said, "That would be a splendid adventure, but I doubt you'd find a cemetery that still had wooden markers. For some strange reason, this one was preserved when most others rotted away or were burned or replaced."

After discussing our ideas, he suggested that we donate the marker to the Maine Historical Society, which owned the Longfellow House in Portland. "If you'd like, I'll make a call and take you two over there later this week, to present your treasure," he offered.

Christopher looked at me and I looked at him.

"I guess that's the second best place for it to be," he said, shrugging.

"Did you make any other progress on your treasure hunt?" Papa asked.

Grammie looked sympathetic when I said "No." Especially when Christopher shook his head.

My friend climbed onto his bike, promising, "I'll stop by Grampie's house today," and rode off to deliver newspapers.

Chapter 25

Tap!

Tap!

Tap!

Something was rapping at my window and it woke me up from a restless sleep. I'd been dreaming of dogs haunting pirates' graveyards and faces leering at me from the trunks of apple trees, so I was kind of glad for an excuse to wake up and get out of bed. I opened the window and stuck my face to the screen to look outdoors.

"Betsy! Come down!" A voice whispered to me out of the darkness.

Staring into the night, I saw a figure holding a bicycle staring back up at me.

"Chris?"

"Shhh! Come down!"

I grabbed my housecoat and slowly opened my bedroom door, listening for any noise from anywhere else in the house. I could hear my grandfather muttering in his sleep in his bedroom and the rest of the house was black and silent. I tiptoed down the stairs, into the kitchen, and out the back door.

"What's the matter?" I whispered.

"Come with me."

Christopher silently dropped his bike, grabbed my hand, and started hurrying me down Shawmut Street.

"Why are you outdoors in the middle of the night?" I whispered again.

"Helping my father load the boat. He and my brothers are going farther out to sea, so they needed an earlier start," Christopher told me. "I was headin' home when I noticed a new boat in Mr. Sullivan's yard. I stopped to admire it and saw something you might want to know about."

The full moon was still a long ways from the horizon. I couldn't imagine what Christopher's surprise was or why I had to see it in the middle of the night. It was kind of exciting to be flitting around town in my pajamas and housecoat on a warm moonlit night. It felt as if we were the only people in the world.

As we headed down the hill at a run, I tripped on a rock and stubbed my toe. I hopped up and down, moaning.

"Shhh!"

That boy had probably never stubbed his toe in his life, I thought to myself, trying not to act like a sissy any more than I had to. He pulled my hand again and we ran. When we reached Mr. Sullivan's driveway, we slowed down and started tiptoeing.

"Wow! That's a nice-looking boat," I said, trying to sound knowledgeable about something I didn't know anything about.

"Look again, Betsy!"

I did as I was told. I choked.

The boat was swamped in moonlight and a figure all in white was sitting in it, swinging an oar over the side.

For a quick minute, I thought that I was seeing my first real, live ghost. Then I realized something. The figure was the shape of my great-grandmother and it was definitely her long, cottony, white hair blowing in the breeze.

I *was* seeing a real *live* ghost!

* * *

My 93-year-old Great-Grammie was piloting a ghostly boat in the moonlight?

"How did she get here? How did she climb up that high?" I asked in awe. I didn't think I could have done it without help.

"That's some great-grandmother you've got!" Christopher marveled.

I followed him to the big boat, which seemed even bigger because it was perched up high on a boat trailer. As Christopher tried to figure out how to climb up, I called out softly to the old, old lady.

"Great-Grammie! Great-Grammie Henley! What are you doing?"

The old lady stopped swinging the oar and looked down at me, then turned to the other side of the boat and saw Christopher's head peering up at her.

"Thank heavens!" she exclaimed. "I thought we'd miss the tide tonight, but you're both here. I was afraid we'd have to come back for you another night. Elizabeth is all ready to go." She held up her worn doll baby so I could see her. "Hoist the sail, Steve! Climb aboard, Erolyn," she ordered, then returned to her rowing.

I got a funny shiver down my back. For one thing, this boat was sitting on a trailer on dry land. For another, this was a fancy motorboat without a sail or mast. And for a third thing, the skipper was a ninety-three-year-old woman!

"Great-Grammie! You have to come down from there! This boat isn't on the water and this isn't the Reach! We're in South Portland!" I whispered, begged, ordered, and argued, but she didn't pay any attention to me. Her face was heading into the night's warm breeze, her heart was heading toward Deer Isle, and the moon had turned us all to a ghostly, silvery white color. I began to feel as if I was in one of those Alfred Hitchcock movies I'd heard about—and my mother never let me watch scary movies.

Christopher hauled himself into the boat and sat down next to my great-grandmother. "Great-Grammie Henley, it's time to go home now," he told her quietly, putting his arm around her shoulder.

"I know, Steve! That's what I've been tellin' you and Erolyn for so long. We must go 'cross the Reach tonight, not bye 'n' bye!" The old lady turned to the boy she thought was her brother and laid her head on his shoulder. "It's been so very long and I'm so very tired," she said with a sigh.

"What do we do now?" I hissed from the driveway.

"I think you've got to go get your grandfather. I don't know how to get her down from here, even if she'd come with us willingly."

I turned and ran home as fast as I could. By the time I'd pounded my way up the stairs, my grandparents were standing in the upstairs hall looking bewildered, with their hair all messed up.

"Grammie! Papa! Great-Grammie's run away again and she's on a boat!" I nearly shouted, I was so excited and upset.

Without a word, Papa ran into the bedroom to get dressed. My grandmother zipped her purple housecoat and ran a hairbrush through her curls. I dashed into my room to find my flip-flops.

"Do we walk or drive?" Papa asked.

"We can walk. The boat is at Mr. Sullivan's house."

"Sully's house? There isn't any water there," Papa said, staring at me.

"I know! That's the point!" I started to run and they hurried behind me as fast as they could.

"Good heavens!" Grammie exclaimed when she saw the white figure swinging an oar off the side of the landlocked boat.

"Who's in the boat with her?" Papa asked.

"Christopher! He's the one who found her here."

Well, if I thought it had taken a lot of talking and cajoling to get Great-Grammie out of the water that day at the beach, it took a *lot* more to get her out of this boat in the middle of the night. We stood there for hours, whispering, talking, pleading, and urging. The sun had begun to peep over the horizon and color the sky pink before we managed to coax the old lady down the ladder Papa had found lying beside Mr. Sullivan's garage. And, just like the last time we led her away from the water, Great-Grammie covered her face with her old, gnarly hands and sobbed.

I know we all felt terrible, but I think maybe Christopher and I felt the worst because we were the ones who had found her and made her leave her dream behind. It was a long, sad walk back to the gray-shingled house on Shawmut Street. Christopher walked on one side of Great-Grammie with his arm around her shoulder and I walked on the other side, holding her hand and the doll she called Elizabeth.

Chapter 26

My parents had taught me to respect my elders and not to argue, but I was arguing the next morning when Christopher appeared at the back screen door with the morning paper.

"Grammie! Papa! We *have* to take Great-Grammie across the Reach and back to Deer Isle!" I was pleading, using the same kind of voice I'd used when I'd tried to get my parents to take me with them this summer. And it had the same effect on my listeners. None whatsoever.

"Elizabeth Henley Sherman, there is nothing I wouldn't do for my mother if I thought it was good for her, but you'll just have to believe me when I say that taking Mama home is not a good idea," Grammie insisted.

Then she said the thing that I hate grown-ups saying: "End of discussion."

I looked at Papa and he raised his eyebrows and nodded. "Betsy, it's not that we haven't considered the idea dozens of times, but we both agree that it's better for Great-Grammie if she stays here, where she's comfortable."

As Christopher watched silently, I launched into the next round of my arguments. "But she's not comfortable! She's unhappy! Maybe she forgot something there. Maybe there's something she needs to do. Or maybe there's someone she needs to see. She has to go home!" Just saying the word *home* made my eyes water and my bottom lip tremble, but I hoped that no one would notice.

At that minute, I knew just how Great-Grammie felt. It makes me so mad and sad at the same time when people say they're doing something for your own good and you know it isn't! It doesn't matter that you know they love you and that they believe what they're saying is true.

"Please, please, can't we go? Only for a day? Maybe if she just sees her old farmhouse, she'll feel better and she'll stop running away!"

"Betsy, it's an eight-hour trip by car. It's impossible to go for a day," Papa said, trying to be reasonable. "But the bottom line is this: we think that going back to her home will make Great-Grammie unhappy."

"How could it? She'd be going home, to the place she loves!"

"It's a very long story, Betsy, and I'm not prepared to argue any longer." My wonderful grandmother rubbed her forehead like it hurt. I could tell by the dark circles under her eyes that she was tired. But she was being so stubborn and I didn't understand why. I knew she loved her mother—I could tell by everything she did for her—so why was she so stubborn about this?

"Betsy, I need to see you outside," Christopher whispered.

"I can't go yet," I told him, sticking my chin out and crossing my arms. But, to my surprise and disgust, he grabbed my arm and dragged me out of the kitchen without saying another word.

"Chris! I—," I protested, ready to put up a fight, but the boy just shook his head and put his finger across his lips.

"What—?"

"Betsy, you're not getting anywhere in there with your arguments. You're just hurting your grandparents' feelings. Nancy Drew would find another way to get where she wanted to go," he argued.

I opened my mouth to argue some more, but shut it right away. When it came to knowing what to say and how to say it, I realized that he was a lot better at it than I was. But I hated to admit that. I clamped my teeth together and glared at him.

* * *

"I'm not saying that I don't agree with you, but let's think of another way to get Great-Grammie to Deer Isle," he suggested.

I looked at him blankly.

"Let's go see your Great-Aunt Elizabeth," he said.

I hadn't thought of her and I should have! She had a fancy Cadillac and a lot of time on her hands if she wasn't entertaining her sewing circle or bridge club. She was the perfect person to take Great-Grammie to Deer Isle!

"Get your bike," Christopher ordered.

We rode across South Portland as fast as we could pedal. On the way, Christopher told me about the story his grandfather had told him about my grandmother and the outhouse.

"He said that your grandmother was the best kid—boy or girl—he ever knew for dreaming up funny jokes," Chris began. "When she was our age, the sheriff of South Portland—who was her neighbor down Shawmut Street—used to walk out his front door and across the porch in his underwear every morning to get his newspaper. For a Halloween prank one year, she talked a gang of boys into moving his outhouse from his back-yard up onto his porch, with the outhouse door open, facing his front door. I guess the mayor was sleepy that morning and walked straight into the outhouse without realizing it. Your grandmother had rigged the door so it shut tight behind him and locked. He couldn't get out for a long time, even though he yelled and hollered. He was finally rescued—in his under-wear—by the minister's wife, who was walking to church. Of course, the kids were in the bushes, watching and laughing.

"I guess he never appeared in public in his underwear again!" Chris said with a grin, looking at me.

I'd been feeling kind of grumpy at my grandmother—and was feeling badly about that. But when I laughed at her tricks, my grumpiness vanished. I was proud of having a grandmoth-er with such a good imagination—and I secretly wished that I could think of such great things to do.

* * *

"Wow!" Chris whistled when we stopped in front of my great-aunt's house on Scammon Street and parked our bikes.

Great-Aunt Elizabeth lives in a big old rambling Victo-rian mansion with turrets and porches decorated with fancy wood trim all around them. She loves gardening as much as my grandmother does, so the yard is full of flowers that smell good.

"I've never been inside such a big house," he said, and he seemed to drag his feet a little at the idea of doing it now.

"Well, Betsy! Christopher! What a lovely surprise!" My great-aunt opened the door wide, and her sunshiny smile was almost as wide.

Although I wanted to blurt out our errand right away, Chris-topher kept giving me warning signs with his face. Finally, when she'd offered us raspberry squares on delicate china plates and lemonade in fancy cut-glass glasses, I couldn't stand it any longer.

"Great-Aunt Elizabeth, do you know where your mother was last night?"

She looked startled and almost dropped the plate she was holding.

"Don't tell me she ran away again?" she exclaimed.

"Christopher found her at three in the morning, rowing a boat that was sitting on top of a boat trailer in Mr. Sullivan's driveway," I told her. "It took me and Grammie and Papa and Christopher the rest of the night to convince her that the boat wasn't going across the Reach!"

My great-aunt's twinkly eyes filled with tears and she reached for her fancy handkerchief.

"We think she needs to go home, ma'am," Christopher told her quietly.

All my great-aunt could do was cry.

"I've thought and thought about that, but in the end I have to agree with Esther and Frank," she said at last.

"But, Aunt Elizabeth!" I moaned. I was so frustrated at all these grown-ups that I couldn't even begin to come up with a good argument. Christopher, who was sitting next to her and out of her line of vision, suddenly made another funny face at me and put his finger across his lips.

"Ma'am, is there anything dangerous about that place that we should know about?" he asked.

"Oh, goodness me! No! It's about the safest, friendliest place in the world," my great-aunt said, offering him more raspberry squares, which, I noticed, he accepted very willingly.

For the next half hour, I sat in my chair and sulked and Christopher kept Great-Aunt Elizabeth talking about how to get to the island from Portland, the bridge that crosses the Reach, the country road that twists and turns through a tiny village on the way to Sunset, the white clapboard houses that line the road, and exactly where Knowlton Lane turns off to the right.

"I have some pictures I could show you," she said, and she walked into the parlor and pulled a black photo album off one of her bookshelves. It was full of a whole lot of black-and-white pictures of the old-fashioned days.

"Most of these people are long gone," my great-aunt sighed, flipping through the pages until she reached the picture of a cozy-looking old white farmhouse and its outbuildings, surrounded by gardens and orchards.

"Who's that sitting on the roof of that shed?" I asked, pointing to a picture of a pretty girl with braids wound around her head and long skirts that reached to the tops of high-button shoes.

"That's your grandmother!"

"Why is she on a roof?" I asked.

"Where *didn't* she climb?" Great-Aunt Elizabeth said, kind of proudly, I thought. "Mama used to say that Esther was part monkey. From the time she was a baby, if you didn't know where she was, you'd look up and find Esther high in a tree, dangling from a ship's mast, crawling across a cliff, hanging from a church steeple, or straddling the ridgepole of somebody's barn. She was a natural-born athlete, I guess you'd say. She had no sense of fear—I inherited enough fears for the two of us."

Gee. It was hard to picture my grandmother doing all those things, but I liked the girl she had been—and would have liked to have had her as a friend.

"Your mother must've been like her, if she can still climb high into boats and run for miles," Christopher pointed out.

160

"I think you're right," Great-Aunt Elizabeth said with a smile and a shake of her head.

"This is a picture of Mama," she said, turning another page.

"She looks just like my mother!" I said in surprise, staring at the familiar smiling brown eyes that were staring back at me from the old picture. They even had the same dimples at the same places in their cheeks, I noticed.

"Great-Grammie Henley was pretty," Christopher said, staring at the picture, then glancing at me and back to the picture. After a minute, he changed subjects.

"Do you have other pictures of the farm at Sunset?"

Great-Aunt Elizabeth turned more pages in the album and we saw what the farm looked like many years ago, covered in snow, covered in apple blossoms, covered in maple leaves, and surrounded by spring flowers. "It's a beautiful place, but nothing fancy. It's small and homey and unpretentious," my great-aunt said with a faraway smile. "The Knowltons were never rich people, but no one ever left there hungry or unhappy or without a coat if our family could help it."

"Is it hard to find?" he asked.

Gee, that boy sure did take an interest in old houses, I thought to myself. That kind of surprised me.

"Heavens, no. It's the first house on the right after you turn down the lane. It looks out over the cove. There are only a handful of neighbors until you reach Sunset Point, and most of them are distant cousins," my great-aunt said.

Christopher and I looked at the whole picture album about Deer Isle before getting up, thanking her, and heading back to my grandparents' house. I'd never known that boy to ask so many questions. Maybe I was rubbing off on him.

"Chris, why—?" I started to ask why he'd stopped me from

asking Great-Aunt Elizabeth to drive us all to Deer Isle, but I didn't get very far.

"Betsy, do you have your notebook in your bike basket?"

When I told him I did, he pulled his bike over to the curb, climbed off, and ordered, "Start writing."

"What? Why?" I had no idea what he was talking about.

"Let's write down everything we know about the Reach and Great-Grammie's house and how to get there."

"Why?" Gee, I was beginning to sound like a record when the needle sticks on my Papa's Victrola.

"Just write."

I scribbled as Christopher listed on his fingers everything we knew: "Key hangs on nail under first step of side porch…food and firewood in the kitchen…three miles from the village, heading due west…first house on right down Knowlton Lane…"

I was impressed at his memory, but I wasn't sure why we needed to write everything down. "Chris, if my grandparents or great-aunt take us there, they'll know how to get to the house. And I don't think they're going to take us," I pointed out.

"Maybe Great-Grammie will find someone else to take her," he said, staring at me.

My jaw must have dropped down to my belly button.

"What are you talking about? Who could take her?" I demanded to know.

Christopher shrugged his shoulders. "My brothers can drive. Maybe they can borrow my grandfather's truck. My father sometimes goes fishing Down East; maybe he could take her on his boat."

"But my grandparents won't take her themselves. Do you really think they'd let her go without them?"

"That's an idea, anyway," he argued, adding, "Do you want her to go or not?"

I nodded my head and returned to my note-taking while my thoughts raced a mile a minute.

"Now, don't say anything more to your grandparents—you don't want to hurt their feelings. They believe they're doing what's right for Great-Grammie," Christopher cautioned me when we were pretty close to the gray house on Shawmut Street.

"But—!"

"Betsy, not everything has to be argued face-to-face right away," he said with a grown-up kind of sigh. "My mother always says that a stew tastes a lot better if it simmers for awhile instead of boiling."

I didn't have any idea what he was talking about, but I didn't want him to know that, so I just nodded my head.

"I've got to go do the papers. Don't say anything until I ask around," he cautioned.

Chapter 27

I waited for a long time outside Great-Grammie's room, watching the little old lady rock, rock, rock hard and fast in the creaky old rocking chair. Her knuckles were white as they clutched the arms of the chair and she wasn't humming this time.

After awhile, I picked up the old doll Great-Grammie called Elizabeth, which was carefully seated in the second, littler rocker, and wedged my bottom onto the seat, sitting the doll in my lap. Then I began rocking to the rhythm of my great-grandmother's chair. My hands clutched the arms of my chair just like hers clutched her chair.

It's kind of spooky when you imitate someone else. Sometimes it can make you believe that you actually can see through their eyes or hear through their ears. If you do it just right, you begin to think differently and look at the world differently. That's what happened to me that afternoon.

The semidarkness of my great-grandmother's tiny little room gave me a safe, sleepy kind of feeling at first. After a while, though, I began to wonder if the walls were very slowly coming closer to me. I wondered if I rocked there long enough if they would box me in, away from all the world. Then I turned to the light.

Through the big open window, I looked out over the wideness and the blueness of the ocean and on to the horizon, and even farther, to the sky. The outside world seemed so big and open and free—and a little bit scary. The longer I looked, the more I could understand what Christopher meant when he said that the ocean calls to people. Sometime in my rocking, I began to think about how great it would be to climb onto the window sill and soar out into the big, wide blue. I didn't want to feel safe any longer. I wanted to feel *free*.

"Erolyn!"

I was so lost in my thoughts that the doll and I jumped when I heard Great-Grammie's voice. I turned back into Betsy again and I wondered: If someone had looked at my eyes when I was rocking, would they have looked like the doll's, painted on and unseeing? Just like my great-grandmother's eyes?

"Yes, Great-Grammie?"

Without looking at me, she declared in a clear, strong voice (just like a grown-up, not like a worn-out old lady with memory problems), "Erolyn, we need to go. These are nice people, but I can't stay here any longer. Don't you understand?"

For the first time, I really did.

"What will you find there, across the Reach, Great-Grammie?" I asked after a long time, as we rocked and looked out the window together.

She didn't answer.

* * *

I don't know how long I sat and rocked in Great-Grammie's room, shifting my eyes back and forth from the darkened walls to the wide, blue world outside. It might have been just a few minutes, or it might have been all afternoon. By the time the rocker stopped and I got up and gently put the doll named Elizabeth in my place, I knew deep in my heart that somehow I had to get my great-grandmother across the Reach and back to her home. Without figuring it out, I also somehow knew that I wouldn't just be doing it for her sake. I would be doing it for me, too.

Though I didn't understand why right then.

But how could an eleven-year-old girl get a ninety-three-year-old woman all the way up the coast all alone?

Maybe Christopher would bring me the answer.

* * *

Late that afternoon, Papa offered to take us all on a drive around the cape and to visit with his friend Mr. Dyer, so we weren't home when Christopher arrived with the newspaper. When we returned, I went to bed early, but I could barely sleep that night, trying to picture different ways we could smuggle my great-grandmother onto Mr. Knight's boat or into Chris's grandfather's pickup truck.

I needn't have bothered, though, because when I cornered Christopher outside the back porch early the next morning, he sighed and said, "My father's not fishing near Deer Isle until fall and my grandfather's truck needs a new transmission."

The two of us sat on the stoop of the garden shed with our heads in our hands, thinking hard.

But the answer arrived two days later.

Chapter 28

My grandmother's cousin, Miss Emmaline Parrott, is a very large woman with a very large voice and very strong opinions. She came to see us Thursday afternoon on her once-a-year trip to visit her old hometown and all her Maine relatives. In the three hours she sat in my grandparents' backyard sipping lemonade and wolfing down thin slices of orange refrigerator cake, she insisted that my grandmother should rearrange her entire garden, repaper the house with "modern" wallpaper, repave the driveway, redecorate the parlor with Modern Danish (whatever that is) furniture, and re-educate me.

"The girl lives in the God-forsaken Midwest. That's no place to raise a child! Corn, maybe, but not children. As much as I love Eliza and admire Charles, they must be told at once to come back East," Cousin Emmaline declared as I looked at her in surprise. Everyone in the Midwest thinks *that's* the only place to raise children.

Grammie and Papa seemed to have figured out that there's

no arguing with people like Cousin Emmaline, so Grammie just tried to change the subject.

"How was the Greyhound bus trip?" she asked, with a glance (and maybe a wink) in Papa's direction.

"Fine. Clean, well-maintained accommodations. A pleasant-enough driver. He pulled into the station three minutes late, but I'd rather be safe than on time—although I did speak to the manager about the lack of punctuality," Cousin Emmaline said, checking her watch to see if she was still being punctual. Then she added something that caught my attention and made me really listen hard.

"I'm taking the bus up to your mother's neck of the woods, Esther. I'll visit with Cousin Berkeley Henley, who left Norway, Maine, to settle nearer the coast, don't you know? There's a Greyhound connection that will take me directly to Blue Hill and I understand that the same bus actually delivers passengers to the foot of the Deer Isle bridge these days. Haven't times changed? It seems as though the world might start making a beeline for islands, now."

I almost jumped up from my seat to run and report the news to Christopher, but I figured that my grandparents would get suspicious—and that Cousin Emmaline would think my behavior was more evidence of the fact that Midwestern children aren't well-bred. So I sat as quietly as I could, trying not to wiggle in the chair. While Cousin Emmaline reported in great detail on the health and care of her three cats, my mind raced a bus up and down the coast of Maine.

Those were the three longest hours of my life, but at last Cousin Emmaline heaved herself to her feet and told Grammie one more time to remember to buy modern wallpaper and Modern Danish furniture. She pinched my cheek (I *hate* it when grown-ups do that!) and said, "Well, at least your parents were smart enough to give you Henley looks." Then she climbed into Papa's car and he drove her off to Cousin Mary Elizabeth Henley's house, where she would be arriving punctually and spending the night.

"Whew!" Grammie said, when the car slowly turned the corner down by Mr. Sullivan's house. "As Cousin Emmaline sat talking, she reminded me of her mother—a startling resemblance! Suddenly, after all these years, I realized why her father was a seagoing man who took very long voyages!" Then she winked at me and carried the lemonade glasses into the house.

I couldn't wait until Christopher brought the afternoon paper so that we could talk about the Greyhound bus idea, but to my surprise, it was the boy named Nick who arrived that afternoon with Christopher's canvas newspaper bag draped over his shoulders.

"What are *you* doing here?" I'm afraid I wasn't very polite. I had too much to discuss with Christopher to worry about any other boy.

"Chris has chicken pox—his whole family does. Everyone but his parents," the boy said in his croaky voice, kind of shyly.

"Oh, NOOOO!" I howled.

* * *

"Grammie, how long does chicken pox last?"

The screen door slapped shut behind me with a terrific *BANG*!

"It's several days before children stop being contagious and it can be weeks before the last spots disappear. That's a very long and uncomfortable illness. Why do you ask?"

Weeks? WEEKS!!! I didn't have weeks to wait for the chicken pox to make its way through the whole Knight family! In twenty days, I'd be sitting on a train bound for Chicago!

When I told Grammie that Christopher and the other Knight kids had the chicken pox, Grammie shook her head and said, "Oh, that poor woman!"

That very afternoon, Grammie set to work baking and chicken-noodle-soup-making. She sent me to the Red & White Grocery around the corner for a long list of things I'd never bought before, like oatmeal soap and calamine lotion. "We'll take these to Bertram Knight's house and he can deliver them to the family," she said.

"Could we buy them some peanut butter and Marshmallow Fluff, too?"

Grammie nodded her head and added them to her shopping list. After wheeling the groceries home in Christopher's old red wagon that he'd left at the house, we loaded them into a box. I wrote Chris a quick letter begging him to get better soon, but I didn't say anything about the Greyhound bus route. I wanted to tell him about my great Plan in person.

I wanted him to be impressed.

Chapter 29

"Grammie, I'm going treasure hunting," I announced the next day, hoping that if I could find the treasure chest full of gold, new bikes would make all the Knights get better faster. During a long and lonely morning and afternoon of digging, I didn't find anything better than a colony of crabs, a handful of sea glass, a dilapidated plastic soldier, and a sad trip home.

I didn't go again.

Life on Shawmut Street wasn't fun after Christopher took sick. I rode my old bike around South Portland and sometimes caught sight of those pesky boys in the distance, but the days seemed very quiet and very long. I worried about how fast time was moving and how slowly my plans for Great-Grammie were moving. When you've had a best friend and he goes away, you learn that adventures are much more fun when you share them with someone—even when that someone always seems so much righter than you are all the time.

Every day I begged and pleaded with Grammie to call

Christopher's house and see how he was doing. All she would say is that his mother had enough on her hands without having to answer the phone all day long. When I kept begging, she finally agreed to call his grandfather for a progress report.

"That boy is probably the worst of the bunch," Mr. Knight told Grammie. "He's covered in pox and running a high fever."

I finally made a little progress on my Plan. One afternoon Papa offered to drive his "three young ladies" into Portland to shop at Porteous Mitchell. While Grammie helped Great-Grammie get ready, I hurried to the phone book and found the address for the Greyhound bus station. After Papa drove away, leaving Grammie, Great-Grammie, and me in front of the huge department store, I did something I'd never done before.

I told a lie.

"Grammie, could I go to Longfellow's Bookstore while you and Great-Grammie shop?" I asked, looking as innocent as I could, but feeling like a crook inside.

Grammie hesitated, then nodded. "Be very careful, Betsy. And always remember, if you are lost or need help, ask a policeman," she reminded me.

I felt like a very guilty Nancy Drew as I ran down the sidewalk with the bus station address clutched tightly in my hand.

"Excuse me, sir. Can you please tell me the way to the Greyhound station?" I asked an old man who was leaning up against a light post. He didn't say anything, just nodded and pointed me down a side street.

The Greyhound station wasn't as clean as my kitchen back home, but it was painted the same color aqua and it had a lot of chrome and Naugahyde seats. I tapped my foot and counted my very fast heartbeats while I waited for the line to move up to the window. My head barely reached above the little shelf by the ticket seller, so I had to stand on my tiptoes.

"Excuse me, sir, can you please tell me what time buses leave for Deer Isle and how much the tickets are?" I asked in my most grown-up voice.

The man behind the bars leaned forward and peered down at me. He was wearing a striped shirt spotted with coffee stains, a very old-looking brown tie, and suspenders. He hadn't shaved that day and he was smoking a smelly old cigar that he moved from one side of his mouth to the other when he answered me.

"The only bus leaves at eight in the morning Mondays, Wednesdays, and Fridays. It's a ten-hour trip, with a change in Camden," he kind of growled at me. I guess I didn't look like a good customer.

The time was okay with me. But the price wasn't! Each ticket would cost more money than I had managed to save from my allowances all summer long.

"Is there any discount for an eleven-year-old kid?" I asked, with my fingers crossed behind my back.

"Half price," he grunted.

Well, that was a little better, but where would I get enough money for Great-Grammie's ticket, let alone mine?

I felt like crying as I dragged my sandals up the bus route and down Congress Street. I had less than two weeks left. My best friend had the chicken pox. My Great-Grammie needed to go to her faraway home. And I was her only hope.

What could I do about all this?

These were more problems than an eleven-year-old girl could handle right now.

I ran into and out of Longfellow's Bookstore, so I wouldn't be living a total lie.

That night, I lay in bed with my arms crossed behind my head for a very long time, trying to think. Only one sort-of-idea came to me in the middle of the night. I remembered how those five boys had promised me that they'd help me if they could.

But how could they help?

Chapter 30

The answer came to me the next day when Nick arrived with the newspaper. Our meeting was almost a repeat of the way I'd gotten to know Christopher.

"Whaddaya doin' up there?" the red-headed boy called up to me after he'd delivered the newspaper. I'd climbed up my grandparents' tallest tree and I had my spyglass to my eye, looking out to sea and wondering how far beyond the horizon Deer Isle floated.

I looked down at him.

"Spyin'," I said.

He shimmied up the tree and followed the direction of my spyglass with his eyes. "What do you see that I can't?" he asked.

I handed him my spyglass and he spent a lot of time looking around in every direction.

"Wow! This is pretty nifty," he said, when he handed it back to me. "I'd sure like to have one like it."

"Pirates use spyglasses just like this," I told him in a nice kind of voice. "In fact, Bluebeard might have used this very spyglass sometime. At least that's what the gift shop clerk told me when I bought it."

He nodded and I could tell he was impressed.

I glanced at his Red Sox hat. "You a Sox fan or do you just wear their hat?" I asked, feeling kind of shy, but also kind of desperate. I really missed talking to a kid my age.

"Are you kiddin'? My whole family loves the Sox! We go to Fenway Park every summer to see a game because my dad's boss gives him tickets."

We talked about batting averages and rookies and MVP's and the American-versus-National leagues for a while, and I told him about my baseball card collection.

"Wow! You're the first girl I ever knew who likes the same things boys like," he said, looking at me as if I was a cat in a terrarium.

"There are more of us than you think," I said, wondering if he meant that as a compliment or complaint.

"No kiddin'?" he asked, shaking his head. "All my sisters want to talk about or play with are Tiny Tears dolls and bunny rabbits." I winced at that, but kept my mouth shut.

And then I got my Idea. My beautiful, brilliant, awful Idea.

"Say! Would you like to see my baseball cards and some other things I brought with me all the way from Chicago?" I asked.

"Sure!" he said, and he sounded excited.

"You can ask your friends if you'd like," I added, as the idea grew in my mind. "I'm thinking of having a sale."

"Why?" He sounded kind of suspicious.

"I've collected so many great things this summer that I'm not sure I can get everything home," I lied. (Boy, my second lie and I wasn't caught this time, either.) Just to convince him a little more, I said, "You know, Christopher and I have been searching for pirate treasure all summer and we've found some pretty interesting stuff."

Well, that boy's eyes grew as big as a baseball. "Where do you want to meet?" he asked.

I didn't want my grandparents to know what I was doing, so I thought quickly and said, "The old school on Cottage Road. Six-thirty."

Nick climbed down the tree—not as fast as Christopher could, I noticed—and headed off on his shiny bike to spread the word.

* * *

Back in Chicago, I'm not a salesgirl. I love everything about Girl Scouts except for selling cookies. I don't like to ask people to buy things. I don't like taking orders. I don't like collecting money. I hate Januarys, when the order forms are handed out at our troop meetings and our leader gives us a pep talk about how every sale benefits our troop and our camping trips. I always beg my parents just to take the form to work—"Scientists need good food, brain food," I always remind them.

But, in Maine, I discovered that I actually have some talent in selling things. The problem was, I was selling things that I didn't want to sell, things that I loved.

At the end of the meeting at the park, I'd sold my Mickey Mouse alarm clock to Danny's kid brother, my SUPERMAN! comic books and secret decoder ring to Sam, my copy of *Treasure Island* to his friend Jack (no one bid on *Anne of Green Gables*—"Ooh! a girls' book!" the boys said all together in disgust.). I convinced Nick to buy *Nancy Drew and the Secret in the Attic* for his sister's birthday present, sold my Roy Rogers gun and holster to Bobby, my compass and Swiss Army knife to Danny, and my spyglass and precious baseball cards to Nick. Daddy would probably ground me for the rest of my life when he found out, I knew, but I decided not to think about that until I had to. Nick even asked if I'd sell him my book bag. With no treasures but *Anne of Green Gables* and my Tiny Tears doll left, I said yes.

I walked back with tears in my eyes, but money in my pocket. If I'd counted right, I had just enough money for our tickets.

* * *

"Great-Grammie?"

I knelt at the side of my great-grandmother's rocking chair, which once again faced the open window and creaked as it went rocking, rocking, rocking, hard and fast.

"It won't be long now, Great-Grammie," I said.

But she didn't look at me. Her eyes were on the blue that stretched far away outside her window.

* * *

That was a very, very long night.

I cried and cried and cried. I wished that I'd hear the Tap! Tap! Tap! of pebbles against my window, like I once had. But it seemed as though I was the only person in the world awake that night.

I really needed a friend to talk to me and tell me I was doing the right thing. But, instead, I lay there with my loneliness, my Plan, and a humongous sense of guilt. I loved my grandparents very, very much, and I knew they loved and trusted me. Not only had I lied to them, but I was about to do something even more awful.

I was about to kidnap Great-Grammie Henley and take her on a bus trip all the way to Deer Isle. By myself.

180

 # Chapter 31

"Nick?" I caught the temporary paperboy flinging papers on porches half a block from my grandparents' home. He turned around fast to look at me.

"Yeah?"

"Which way do I go to find the bridge to Portland?" I tried to look kind of casual when I asked. Papa had driven me there many times, but I'd never really paid much attention to roads and turns—and I sure was sorry about that now.

"Why do you want to know?" he asked, kind of suspicious. "Why don't you ask your grandparents?

"Because I'll be on a bike and I don't know if there's a better way for bikes than a car would take." (I was getting pretty good at lying, I told myself.)

He narrowed his eyes and looked at me, then shrugged his shoulders and mumbled, "As soon as I deliver the last paper, I'll take you there."

"Gee! Thanks!" I said, finally convinced that there might be a nice kid under the Sox hat.

It was a good thing I had Nick with me, otherwise I would never have found the way. That boy took me through deserted yards, under an overpass, along back alleys, and past deserted parking lots. Finally I caught sight of the bridge.

"Thanks," I said. I must've looked a little worried as I looked at that tall bridge riding so high in the sky. I suddenly remembered my mother saying that heights bother some people and I wondered if I'd be one of them. "Do you think I need to walk my bike over or can I ride it?"

He didn't answer me for a minute, but then he asked something that surprised me. "Do you want me to go with you?"

I didn't answer him right away. I thought about whether I should confide in a goofy stranger. But then I decided that I really needed a friend right now and even if this boy wasn't the one I really, really wanted, he was better than nothing. And I was really glad to have someone go with me.

"I'd like that," I blurted out.

That boy wasn't mean or goofy, like I used to think. He nodded his head, climbed on his bike, and started heading to the bridge. Every once in awhile he turned his head, to make sure I was following behind.

It was a very good thing he did. Otherwise, I'd probably have lost my nerve and turned for home. That bridge was the scariest thing! Cars rushed past us, just inches from our bikes. Boat horns blew loudly in our ears. The bridge was made of metal strips and I could see the water rushing far, far below the tires of my bike. I panicked and wondered if I could fall through the gaps anywhere. But the red-headed boy kept going, so I did, too.

"Where to?" Nick asked, at the end of the bridge.

I didn't want to tell him my secret, but I was shaking because I was so scared—and guilty. I decided to trust him.

"To the Greyhound bus station," I whispered. He had to lean in closer to hear me over the traffic noise.

"It's straight up that hill—and High Street is steep," he warned, starting off again on his bike. As hard as I tried, I couldn't keep up. I had to get off my bike and push it; the hill seemed to rise straight up into the sky. I cringed, thinking he'd laugh at me when he looked back, but he didn't. That boy actually got off his bike and pushed it along beside me.

"Are you goin' back to Chicago soon?" he asked.

"Yup," I said.

I was trying hard not to lie any more than I had to—I was afraid I'd get too good at it and it would be a hard habit to break. I knew he was assuming that I'd be taking the bus back to Chicago, but I didn't set him straight.

"Would you please watch the bikes while I get the tickets— uh, ticket?" I asked when we wheeled to a stop in front of the bus station.

"Ayuh," he said, as he leaned his shiny bike up against my battered and rusty old bike, then sat on the curb and pulled out a half-chewed wad of gum from behind his ear (ych!), which he shoved into his mouth.

"Two tickets for Deer Isle, please. One adult, one eleven year old, leaving tomorrow," I said in my most grown-up voice to the cigar-smoking man at the sales window. This time he was wearing a white shirt, but it was as spotted as the last one had been. He moved the cigar from one side of his mouth to the other and swiveled his head close to the bars of the window, trying to see who I was with, I guess.

"Where's the adult?" he asked.

I don't know why he was suspicious.

"At home," I said, glad I didn't have to lie about that.

I very carefully counted out my pennies, nickels, dimes, and quarters, and realized to my relief that I still had $1.27 when I was done. The man handed me the tickets and warned me, "Be here early. Buses leave right on time."

* * *

Nick was still sitting on the sidewalk, chewing gum and skimming small stones across the street in between cars passing by. He got up right away when he saw me.

"Do you go home all by yourself, too?" he asked.

"No, my parents arranged for a college kid to ride back with me," I said, not bothering to tell him that I'd be going home on a train, not a bus.

"When do you go?"

"In eleven days." I hoped that he wouldn't want to know why I was so anxious to get a ticket today—and why my grandfather wouldn't drive me to the bus station.

"Are all girls in Chicago like you?" he asked, kind of shyly this time.

I wasn't sure how to answer that. "I don't think so," I said, kind of cautiously. I'd never thought about that before. "Everyone else I know has brothers and sisters and mothers who stay home with them."

We walked our bikes back down the steep hill before darting through traffic to get back to the South Portland Bridge. Nick didn't say much for most of the walk, but just at the end, he took a deep breath and said, "I'm sorry we said your great-grandmother was a witch." He didn't look at me when he said it and he kind of shaded his eyes and looked at the horizon as though ignoring the words as well as me.

"Well, she's an awfully sweet little old lady when you get to know her," I started to say in a superior voice. But the boy had been really nice to me, so I decided I'd be honest with him—about this, anyway. "Actually, I was a little afraid of her, too, at first," I confessed. He looked at me in surprise. "My grandmother once said that people today don't have much use for old people and now I understand what she means. My Great-Grammie can do amazing things—climb up into high places, run more than a mile and a half, swim out to offshore islands, and row boats—at ninety-three years old!"

"Wow!" he said. I think he was really impressed.

"But most people ignore her or talk in front of her as if she won't understand what they're saying," I added.

Sometimes I surprise myself when I talk. Ideas come out that I don't even know I have. Getting to know Great-Grammie had been like reaching through clouds, hoping to find a real, whole person inside them. But, even though I often missed what I was reaching for, it had been worth the hard work. And then I suddenly realized something important: this summer I'd grown from someone who was afraid and ashamed of an old lady to someone who was proud of her.

Wow.

* * *

The ride back home seemed a lot faster than the ride to the bus station. I concentrated hard on not falling down through the cracks of the bridge, and Nick could pedal his bike a lot faster than I could, so I struggled to keep up until I got back to Shawmut Street. I was breathing real hard by that time.

"Gee, thanks for your help," I said, kind of awkwardly.

"Sometime could you tell me about your pirate adventures?" Nick looked at me, then looked up and down the street, probably to see if any of the other guys were watching him talk to a girl. When I didn't answer right way, he looked at me again.

"Well, I guess so, but Christopher can talk about pirates better than I can," I said.

We looked at each other out of the corners of our eyes and then I climbed on my bike and said, "I've got to get home before someone misses me. Thanks again!" I waved and I biked away fast.

Chapter 32

Gee, how I missed Christopher! I wanted someone
to tell me I was doing the right thing. And I wanted someone
to help me think through all the things I should think about.
I opened my notebook a dozen times, grateful that Chris had
asked me to write down everything we could remember about
the trip to the old white farmhouse on Knowlton Lane.

I had a lot to think about that afternoon. When my grandparents offered to take me for a ride around the cape, I offered to
watch my great-grandmother instead, so they could go alone.
As soon as the old gray Studebaker pulled out of the driveway,
I hurried into the kitchen and made a pile of fluffernutters and
peanut-butter-and-jelly sandwiches, grabbed some apples and
grapes, wrapped some cookies in waxed paper, poured cold
water into two bottles, and hurried up to my room to hide everything in the suitcase under my bed.

"Great-Grammie, if you go on a trip, what do you take with
you?" I asked the old, old lady as she rocked slowly, humming
her nameless song.

Today the window shades seemed to be pulled right down in front of my great-grandmother's eyeballs and she never did answer me. I decided she'd want her doll Elizabeth, a nightie, change of clothes, her toothbrush, and her hairbrush with her initials on it, but I didn't know what else old ladies would need. I pulled open her drawers and took out some clothes, which I packed with mine. At the last minute, I shoved my Tiny Tears doll into my bag.

Later, when Papa was reading the paper and Grammie was busy making dinner, I snuck my suitcase up to the head of Shawmut Street and hid it in a big thicket of bushes. That would speed up our getaway tomorrow, I thought. I just hoped no one would find it between now and then.

Dinner was very quiet. I don't think that food ever tasted as good or my grandparents ever seemed kinder. About a hundred times I thought about telling them what I was about to do. Another hundred times I came close to crying, thinking about how I was about to disappoint my very special grandparents so badly.

"You're really missing Christopher, aren't you?" Grammie asked, so sympathetically that the tears I'd been fighting spilled over from my eyes.

"Yup," I admitted.

I sat there for the rest of supper trying to figure out how I could get Great-Grammie out of the house early enough in the morning. Then I got a break.

Ring! Ring!...Ring!...Ring!

The voice at the other end of the telephone asked for my grandfather. When Papa hung up, he turned to me and asked a favor.

"Betsy, would you mind watching your great-grandmother

again tomorrow morning? Mrs. Pierce's husband is out of town and she and her family need a ride to the train station to meet him. I think I'll need Grammie to help with all the children."

"Sure!" I said, thinking that I must be doing something right to have one problem solved so easily.

* * *

Dong! Dong! Dong!

I listened to Papa's grandfather clock chime every hour that night. My mind had fifty million things to think about. I was dressed and packed long before the sun came up and I snuck into Great-Grammie's room when I heard her begin to hum. She'd dressed herself in a winter coat and summer sun hat, but I was glad to see that she had her best housedress on underneath and her shoes on the right feet.

"Let's eat a big breakfast today, Great-Grammie," I said, taking her hand and leading her down the stairs when she was ready. "We don't want to be hungry later on."

"Betsy? Why are you up so early?" Grammie called from her bedroom as she fixed her hair in front of the mirror.

"I, well, it's going to be such a hot day," I said, fumbling for an answer that wouldn't include a lie.

I poured us big bowls of Cheerios and big glasses of orange juice, unwrapped yesterday's blueberry muffins, and ate as many as I could stuff down. My great-grandmother ate almost as much as I did. When we were done, my grandparents appeared.

"Have fun together! We'll be back as quickly as we can," they promised.

"Don't hurry," I said—and I *really* meant it.

As soon as I saw the car head out of the driveway, I pulled a note out of my pocket and stuck it on a shelf in my grandmother's spice cupboard, which she usually doesn't open until noon.

We'd be halfway to Deer Isle by then, I reckoned, so that would be a safe place. I put Great-Grammie's doll and purse in her arms, grabbed her hand, and headed out the door.

At last came the best part of the Plan.

"Great-Grammie Henley?" I asked, putting my hands on her shoulders and looking her straight in the eyes. She stared back at me, her face blank.

"We're going across the Reach! I'm taking you home today!"

"The Reach?" she echoed vaguely. Then, a moment later, the message seemed to reach her mind.

"We're goin' 'cross the Reach? Goin' home?" she said again, louder. She clapped her hands and kissed me on the cheek. But then she stopped and asked, worriedly, "But Erolyn, where's Steve?"

That was a problem I should have anticipated. But I was getting pretty good at lying by now.

"He'll meet us there," I said, wishing that my lie wasn't a lie.

By the time Great-Grammie and I had walked the three blocks to the clump of bushes hiding our suitcase, I wasn't feeling as good about what I was doing. Great-Grammie was shuffling slowly, looking in every doorway and garden for Christopher-called-Steve.

I kept wondering if I could remember the route Nick had taken me on yesterday to get to the bus station—and I worried whether a ninety-three-year-old lady could make it that far. I remembered what my nanny had said once about hitchhiking, but I knew that my parents would be horrified if I even thought about doing it. I'd broken about half of the Ten Commandments already, I figured, and I decided to try hard not to break any more of them.

I pulled my great-grandmother along while trying to drag the suitcase (it felt a *lot* heavier than it had last night!) and remember the route in my mind.

And then...a miracle happened.

Chapter 33

"Betsy!"

I twirled around and thought I was seeing a mirage, just like the cowboys in Westerns always see in the desert.

"Christopher?

"Christopher!".

I threw my arms around that boy and hugged him real tight, I was so happy to see him. Then I remembered that he was a boy and I stepped back in a big hurry, with my hands behind my back.

"Steve!"

Great-Grammie did exactly what I'd done. She threw her arms around him, too, but she also kissed him on both cheeks. He smiled when he looked into her eyes, then turned to me and smiled.

Yup, he was just like a lighthouse—always there when you need him.

When I looked closer, I thought Chris seemed a lot skinnier than he had ten days ago. His face and arms still had red spots all over them, but no one had ever looked better to me!

"Chris, are you all right?"

He just nodded.

"You kinda still look sick," I said hesitantly, but he shook his head.

"Chris, you're not going to believe this—" I started to tell him in a rush what was happening, but he cut in.

"You're taking Great-Grammie to Deer Isle yourself," he said matter-of-factly, as if the island was no farther away than Grammie's backyard.

"How did you know?" My eyes felt like they were popping out of my head.

"Nick came by for the papers yesterday afternoon and told me he'd taken you to the Greyhound bus station. I know you took the train from Chicago."

Wow! You can't sneak anything past that best friend of mine, I thought proudly. But he'd just begun to surprise me.

Christopher pulled my book bag, bulging with things, out of the bushes.

"Where did you get that?" I asked. I couldn't believe my eyes!

"Nick also told me about your sale. I figured you needed money for bus tickets."

"Don't tell me he gave all that stuff back to you!"

"I bought it back."

* * *

"You did *what*, Chris?" I was so surprised that I could barely make my mouth work.

"Nobody should have to give up their most special treasures when they're doing a good deed," he said, not really looking me in the eyes. "Anyway, this stuff should come in handy on the trip."

I was so surprised that I sat plunk down on my suitcase. When she saw me do it, Great-Grammie Henley did the same thing. I opened my mouth and closed it, looking up at Christopher like some kind of dumb wooden toy.

"Betsy! We've got to hurry, or we won't get to the station on time!"

He hauled me up by one arm, pulled Great-Grammie Henley up by both hands, pulled the old red wagon out from behind a tree, and then loaded my book bag and suitcase beside another small bag.

"But Chris! Where did you get the money to buy all those things back?" Even knowing that we needed to hurry, I couldn't stop asking questions.

He didn't answer me for a long time. He held my great-grandmother's hand and pulled the wagon while I hiked along beside him. I must have asked the same question four times before he finally muttered something.

"What?" I asked, leaning closer to hear what he'd said.

"Newspaper fund," he muttered.

"But that's for your new bicycle!" I stopped, ready to argue.

Chris must have heard me, but he just kept hurrying along the sidewalk, so I ran to catch up. I was just about to open my mouth and ask more questions when he looked up at the clock on the bank tower and said breathlessly, "We really have to hurry or we're not going to make it!"

"Hurry!" my great-grandmother repeated. I think she finally realized that we were off on our big adventure. I began trotting alongside them.

Suddenly, from a side street, the gang of five appeared. They took one look at us and wheeled up to see what all the action was about. Chris looked at me and then looked at them.

"Remember what you said after Betsy helped you out of Mr. Macomb's garden?" he asked all the boys, but looking Nick hard in the eyes.

"Ayuh," they said, all together.

"We need to get to the bus station by 7:45—can you help?"

"Sure!" they chorused, then went silent, and Bobby said, "How?"

"Can you loan us two bikes and someone who can help with the bags?"

Wow! I couldn't believe how fast Christopher could think. He should have been the captain of a ship or the general of an army or something.

"Sam and Bobby will give you their bikes and the rest of us can carry a bag, but what do we do with the old lady?" Danny asked, turning his baseball hat back-to-front as though he meant business.

"I'll pull her in the wagon behind me. Like I pull my brothers," Chris said.

"I can ride a horse!" Great-Grammie spoke up for the first time, and we all turned and stared at her.

I hurried over and asked, "But Great-Grammie, can you ride a bicycle?"

She just stood there and stared at me, a faraway look in her eye.

Very quietly, Christopher walked up to her, took her hand, and said, "Great-Grammie Henley, we're going to take you home, but first, I have to take you to the bus station. You're going to have to sit in this wagon and hold on. We'll ride to the bus that will take us to Deer Isle.

"But, Steve, I want to ride the horse!" she said stubbornly.

"Grammie, this is part of the adventure! Steve is going to

196

help us get to the Reach!" Desperately, I walked up to her other side and tried to help Chris lift the old lady into the wagon.

Nick saw me struggling and pushed me aside. He lifted her up in his arms as though she was his little sister. With Chris hurriedly roping the wagon to the back of Sam's bike, Nick plunked Great-Grammie into the little red wagon and I helped her fold her legs Indian-fashion. Quickly, three boys grabbed the three bags. Bobby and Sam were left behind in our dust.

Five of us were off, hair flying, tires wobbling, with Danny leading the way.

"Whee!" My great-grandmother shouted. She seemed to be having a fine time on her modern-day horse.

"Where are you going?" Danny yelled at me over his shoulder.

"What's the Reach?" Nick yelled at me from behind my back.

"Who's Steve?" Joey yelled from beside me.

"It's a long story—but we just can't miss this bus!" I gasped for air as I pedaled as fast as my legs would go.

I didn't have time to worry about falling through the grids of the South Portland Bridge this time—I had something else to worry about.

The drawbridge was up and a very slow-moving oil tanker was taking its time heading toward the bridge.

Chapter 34

We all came to a screeching stop as the black-and-white-striped gate dropped down over the foot of the drawbridge. Chris and Nick quickly helped Great-Grammie out of the wagon to stretch her legs, then Christopher grabbed her hand.

"Will we make it on time, Chris?" I asked anxiously, so grateful that I had someone else to help me do the thinking. He nodded, but he never took his eyes off the tanker.

I felt as though I had Mexican jumping beans in my stomach. My face and hands were all sweaty and my head felt like a teakettle about to boil. I looked at Chris, but his jaw was shut tight, his eyes were concentrating on the water, and he seemed to be counting the inches the tanker had to go before it left the bridge behind. Great-Grammie stood beside him, smiling, looking at the water and holding her doll.

As long as we were waiting, I started answering some of the boys' questions. I explained about the Knowlton home at Sunset and how my great-grandmother needed to go there. Fortunately, there wasn't enough time for someone to ask me why my grandparents weren't going with us. I was too tired to think up any more lies.

"Get ready to ride!" Christopher shouted as the drawbridge slowly creaked downward. We were off like racers as soon as the striped arm started swinging upward.

The three boys managed to ride their bikes up that very high High Street at the end of the bridge, but I knew I couldn't do it and Chris couldn't do it pulling my great-grandmother in the wagon behind him. We helped Great-Grammie out of the wagon. While Chris dragged our bikes and the wagon, I took Great-Grammie's hand and pulled her up the hill as fast as she could go. At the top, I was nearly wheezing, I was so tired, but the old lady barely seemed out of breath.

The boys had waited for us, and Nick walked up and plunked Great-Grammie back into Chris's wagon. The three rode in front of us like a police escort. We must have been going a hundred miles an hour when we screeched up to the Greyhound station.

The bus had just pulled out of the driveway.

* * *

"Wait! Wait!" I screeched.

I dropped the bike and ran alongside the moving bus, pounding on its side. When the driver hit the brakes and opened the door, I held out the tickets in my hand and breathlessly pointed out, "We have tickets!" The driver looked grumpy, but he nodded, jerked his head in the direction of the back of the bus, and checked his watch.

Then I turned to Chris and the boys and started to thank them.

"I'm going with you," Chris said, holding out his own ticket.

If I live to be ninety-three years old, I'll never forget how surprised and grateful I felt. I should have protested, but I was so glad and so selfish that all I could do was nod and turn back to look at the bus driver.

"Come on! Come on!" he sort of growled, until he saw the row of kids surrounding a tiny old lady with long, cottony, flyaway white hair.

"What the—? Who's—?" he sputtered.

Christopher turned to Danny, Nick, and Joey and held out his hand. Then I did, too. Christopher collected the three bags while I handed my great-grandmother her purse and doll. Then I took Great-Grammie's hands and the boys helped her up the very high steps.

* * *

Great-Grammie must have been tired out by all the excitement because as soon as we settled her in a seat by the window, she hugged her doll, closed her eyes, and sighed.

As soon as I plunked down beside her, I felt kind of shy and very amazed at what we'd just done.

"Chris, I really don't know what to say except thanks," I said, and I felt like crying. "You used your bike money for this. I know you did! I'll repay you as soon as I can. I promise!"

I was so happy that he was there, but so sorry that he'd have to start all over again to earn enough money for his new bike, that I didn't know how to feel.

Chris just looked at me. After a minute, he asked in a quiet voice, "Why didn't you tell me what you were planning?"

I felt swamped with guilt. At that minute I finally realized that having a friend know the secret would have made it a lot easier—and probably a lot better.

"I didn't want to make you feel bad—or maybe I didn't want you to tell me that it wasn't a good idea," I said, after a minute.

Then I added, "*Do* you think it's a good idea?"

He stared at me for a minute. "I do. But I sure hope you remembered your notebook."

"I did!"

Chapter 35

"Want a fluffernutter?"

My watch said that it was only ten o'clock, but my stomach insisted it was way past noon. Lunch sounded really good to Chris and me, it turned out. He put aside my notebook, which he'd been reading and rereading. We wolfed down sandwiches, apples, and a handful of cookies while Great-Grammie slept.

By that time, I'd gotten my courage up to ask Christopher, "What did you tell your parents so they let you go away?"

"The truth. That I was going with you and Great-Grammie to Deer Isle," he said shortly, looking at me while I gawked at him.

"And...they *let* you?"

He grinned and explained, "I guess I forgot to mention that your grandparents weren't going." But I noticed that his cheeks were the pinkest I'd ever seen them. I knew he hated lies, even untold lies.

For the first couple of hours, while Great-Grammie slept with her head resting against the window, it felt exciting to go on a trip with my best friend. Chris said he'd never ridden on a bus before, and the only time I'd ever done it was for a few school field trips, so this was a real adventure for us. We'd never been north of Portland, either—at least, Chris hadn't been north on land, just on water. We spent a lot of time trying to catch glimpses of the ocean and occasional rivers, counting church steeples, and playing the license plate game. The longer the day stretched, the more butterflies began flip-flopping in my stomach.

I began glancing out the window more and more often, wondering if I'd see my grandfather's car passing the bus. Half the time I *worried* that I'd see it; the other half I *wished* I'd see it. Every couple of minutes I put my hands into my pocket and felt around for all the money I had left in the world: $1.27 in twelve pennies, seventeen nickels, and three dimes. Finally, I couldn't stand it any longer.

"Chris?" I asked timidly.

"Chris?" I repeated when he didn't look up from my Nancy Drew book right away. When he did look up, it was reluctantly, I could tell.

"You *do* think we're doing the right thing for Great-Grammie, don't you, Chris?" I asked, trying not to sound pleading.

He looked at me for a long minute before he nodded.

"She needs to go back, Chris! There's something at her home that she needs to see or do," I argued out loud, as though I was rehearsing for the moment when I had to explain to my grandparents—or, worse yet, the *police!*—why I'd kidnapped a ninety-three-year-old woman.

"I know," he said, and he awkwardly patted my hand. Then he glanced at Great-Grammie. We rode. And we rode. And we rode. And we rode. And all the time, Great-Grammie slept, clutching her doll to her chest.

Just when I thought that the ride would never end, the bus lurched to a stop in a sad-looking parking lot, the motor died with a moan, and the driver threw open the bus doors with a squeal.

"Is this Deer Isle?" I asked anxiously. "It hasn't been ten hours yet!"

Christopher inched his way down the aisle, waiting politely for the people ahead of us to get off the bus. Then he spoke to the bus driver, who was already unloading all the baggage from a side compartment on the outside of the big old gray bus. By the time Chris returned, I'd remembered being told that we would change buses somewhere Down East and pick up the seacoast route, so our first bus could head on to Augusta, the state capital.

I gently wiggled Great-Grammie's shoulder.

"Great-Grammie! I'm sorry to wake you up, but we need to get on another bus," I explained, then helped her to her feet and handed her the doll baby she called Elizabeth. I took her hand and she shuffled, shuffled, shuffled slowly, almost painfully, off the bus. She didn't say a word or seem curious about what was happening. I worried that the wild ride to the Greyhound station had been too tiring for her—but she had seemed to enjoy it!

Chris put our bags at my feet. It was a hot day, but I shivered on the corner of the parking lot, waiting for our next bus to arrive. Great-Grammie sank silently onto my suitcase, clutching her doll and gently rocking back and forth, back and forth, humming her nameless tune. Christopher marched in front of us, to the left, then to the right, like a soldier guarding a monument.

Fifteen minutes later, a battered gray bus pulled in front of us and its doors opened with a squeal. I let out a sigh that I'd held in my chest for a really long time.

"Come on, Great-Grammie! This bus is going to take us to Deer Isle!" I grabbed her hand as Chris held her elbow. Together we pulled her up. Silently she hugged her doll to her old bony chest. The driver barely glanced at us after Chris handed him our tickets.

With Great-Grammie between us, we worked our way to the back of the bus. The three of us wedged ourselves into a two-person seat. This time, the bus was empty except for three old ladies about my grandmother's age. Then, the moment before it pulled away, a big family carrying tubes and picnic baskets and bags that probably held bathing suits scrambled on board and sank into the seats behind the driver. I was glad for their loud, happy voices.

This time, the ride seemed even longer. I was sure that my grandparents would be hot on the back tires of the bus and I constantly turned my head, craning my neck to see if I could catch a glimpse of a familiar old gray Studebaker. Chris must have thought the same thing because he finally asked, "Where did you put the note to your grandparents?"

"In the spice cabinet. Grammie usually opens it around noontime when she makes lunch. I thought that would give us enough of a head start," I explained.

I wasn't sure if I was glad or sad that they wouldn't have seen the note earlier. My guilty brain was working overtime, imagining every possible ending to my Plan. Perhaps my grandparents would be so disgusted they would just forget about us and never come. (That was the least possible option, I thought, remembering how much they loved me.) They could call a policeman and have us arrested for kidnapping. (Another thing I didn't *think* they'd do, but they *might* call a policeman to capture us until they could reach us.) Or, they could catch up with us, admit that they were wrong and we were right, and take us the rest of the way to the Knowlton farmhouse. (This was my favorite scene, but I wasn't sure that this would be the way our adventure would end, either.)

Then I had a scary thought: What if they didn't see the note at all? What if Grammie didn't need spices at lunch today? Where else should I have put the note so they wouldn't see it right away, but would definitely see it?

Over and over again, I wanted to ask Chris what he thought might happen—or what he wished would happen—but I didn't want him to know that I wasn't sure about my Plan. After all, it was *my* Plan!

We rode. And I worried.

We rode. And I worried.

We rode. And we rode. And we rode.

Finally, at some point in the afternoon, I fell asleep, with my head sinking onto Great-Grammie's shoulder. We must have looked like a pair of dominos, tilted at the same angle. When Great-Grammie stirred, I woke up, too. I noticed that Chris hadn't made any progress reading Nancy Drew, but I didn't ask what he'd been doing or thinking. I passed around the last of the peanut-butter-and-jelly sandwiches and we chewed silently, all of us lost in our own thoughts—and, in my case, worries. Chris couldn't help but notice the number of times I turned to look out the back of the bus, but he didn't turn and he didn't say anything. He did open the notebook pretty often, though, and he looked as if he were trying to memorize everything it said.

The noisy family left the bus sometime in the middle of the

afternoon and I missed their loud, happy voices. The old ladies left at the next stop. By the time the shadows were lengthening, we were the only ones left on the bus. It seemed like a very long time before at last Chris called, "I see the bridge across the Reach!"

At the sound of his words, I swallowed hard and sat straight up. So did Great-Grammie. It was the first time she'd moved on her own since the bike ride. She sat up with such a jolt that it looked like someone had stuck her with a pin.

"The Reach? The *Reach*?" she squawked. Those were the first words she'd said since we had climbed onto the first bus. Before the driver had even begun to slow down, she had leaped to her feet and was trying to crawl over me.

I grabbed my great-grandmother around the waist as the bus skidded onto the gravel pull-over at the foot of the big green bridge and screeched to a stop. Great-Grammie landed with a *plop!* on my lap. The driver jerked the door open with another a squeal. (Gee, doesn't anyone in the bus service have a can of oil? I wondered. My dad was a stickler for non-squeaky doors and floorboards. Later, I wondered why I thought *that* thought, with all the other things I had to think about!)

"Last stop! All off!" the burly man in the wrinkled uniform bellowed. He turned around and really looked at us for the first time. His voice suddenly dropped like an autumn leaf falling from a tree when he saw the frail old lady clutching her doll and moving as fast as she could down the aisle. Chris had politely stepped aside for the two of us to leave first.

"Hey, kids! Is there someone to meet you here?" the driver asked. Concern suddenly spread across his big, red, kind face. He gently took Great-Grammie's hand and helped her off the bus—kind of like a knight in a fairy tale. (Maybe people who live near islands value old people more than Grammie thinks they do in other places.)

"There will be, sir," Christopher said while I was scrambling in my mind for a way not to lie when there was obviously no car waiting for us.

The driver handed Chris our bags, looked at us curiously, then looked left and right, up and down the road, uncertain about what to do. I could tell he wanted to ask us a lot of questions, but was too polite—or in too much of a hurry—to ask.

"We'll be all right, sir. Thanks!" Chris promised, bending to tie his shoe.

After another look at the road in both directions, the driver shrugged, handed us our three bags, climbed back on the bus, and waved at us after the door squealed shut. When the bus had turned and was about to lurch off the gravel and onto the road, an old black car slowly drove into view. I could see the bus driver glance back at us and point as if to say, "They're here!" before he drove off.

We watched the bus until it disappeared around a corner and the black car until it drove off in the opposite direction.

"Look! There's an eagle's nest on the top of that bridge!" I said excitedly, after we'd gathered our belongings and turned our faces to the bridge across Eggemoggin Reach. I pointed to a giant bird swooping through the air. I'd only seen pictures of eagles and their nests before.

"Osprey," Christopher corrected. Then, when he saw my disappointment, he said, "but they're special birds, too."

Great-Grammie had glided along beside me without saying anything until we reached the foot of the bridge that had been built long after she'd married and left her island. Her head swung restlessly from side to side. I guess she didn't like what she saw. She stopped and focused on a small white building across the water, on the island side, staring for a long time, while Chris stopped to read the sign on the bridge.

Suddenly, my great-grandmother wrenched her hand from mine and began running down the hill to the water.

"The Reach! Elizabeth! Erolyn! Steve! It's the Reach!" she cried.

Chris and I dropped our bags and went scrambling after her until we reached the little landing beach there, tucked under the shadow of the bridge. Across the stretch of water, a big island lined with rocks and big green-blue trees faced us. Sailboats drifted along the horizon.

"Christopher! It's beautiful!" I whispered.

There was something almost magical about that place that rose up out of the ocean water. I'd never seen it before, I'd never even heard of it before this summer, but the whole island seemed to sail right into my heart at that minute. Chris paused with me to look and nod.

By that time, Great-Grammie had managed to crawl into a little motorboat that was pulled onshore beside a big rock.

"Hey! Hey, there! That's my boat!" A big, chunky, yellow-haired boy who might have been fourteen or fifteen came running down the hill, the ends of his green-and-black flannel shirt flapping as he ran. He stopped abruptly when he saw the passenger, who had settled herself on a seat and was holding her doll up in the air, pointing to the island and whispering something.

"Great-Grammie! There's a bridge now! We don't have to take a boat! And, anyway, this isn't our boat!" I pleaded with her, my face burning hot.

"No bridge!" Great-Grammie insisted, shaking her head.

"Great-Grammie, this isn't our boat!" I tried again, remembering with a silent groan how long it had taken us to get my great-grandmother out of Mr. Sullivan's landlocked boat. I turned to Chris for some help and noticed him whispering to the boy.

"It's all right, kid," the boy said to me, after he nodded at Chris. "I'll take you across the Reach so you don't have to walk."

He pushed the boat out a ways into the water and clambered onto the back bench of the boat. Chris threw our bags onto the floor of the boat, then pushed us out farther and splashed up to his knees in seawater before he gently climbed onto the middle seat beside me.

I saw the boy glance curiously over his shoulder at Great-Grammie and her doll before he grabbed the cord and gave the motor a pull to start it. The little old lady and the little old doll paid absolutely no attention to the rest of us. Great-Grammie leaned forward and clutched the edge of the boat, as if she could will us over to the other side without any help from anyone.

A warm breeze seemed to welcome us all home as the motor putt-putted us away from the rocky shoreline and headed us around a point of land and toward the beautiful, long-wished-for island. The quiet rhythm seemed to lull my mind into a kind of dream. My thoughts sailed back to an afternoon when I was a really little kid and my mother had laid down with me to help me take a nap. She'd fallen asleep right away, facing me with her arm thrown over my belly. I laid there for a long, long time, feeling her soft, warm breath on my cheek and watching her chest rise and fall gently, just like the little waves in the Reach rising and falling at this very minute. I remember an overwhelming feeling of happiness and being loved and cared for. That's how I felt now, nestled on that little boat amongst two lobster traps, a coil of rope, suitcases, my best friend, my great-grandmother, an ancient doll, and a complete stranger. That feeling of being cared for didn't seem to have anything to do with the fact that my great-grandmother couldn't think clearly and that I'd known one of these people for three months and one for three minutes.

Like seagulls that always face in the same direction when the wind blows, Chris, the unknown captain of our tiny boat, and Great-Grammie all stuck their faces into the warm breeze in the same direction. Their expressions as we headed across the Reach seemed to suggest that they shared a wonderful, happy secret.

When the motorboat at last pulled up to the shore on the far side of the Reach, the red-faced, yellow-haired skipper turned to Chris and asked, "Who are you folks, anyways?"

It took him long enough!

Chris introduced us, then explained, "We're bringing Great-Grammie home, where she grew up."

"Name?" the boy asked. He sure wasn't a big talker.

"Knowlton," I told him.

"My grandfather's a Knowlton! You've gotta be some sort of relative," he said, looking directly at my great-grandmother, who hadn't paid him any attention at all.

He leaped out of the boat and splashed to its head. The boy hauled us, boat and all, up onto the shore, then carefully handed Great-Grammie out. Her old-fashioned high-heeled shoes splashed in the shallow water, but she didn't seem to notice because her eyes were staring at the tops of the trees ahead of us. Chris shook our captain's hand and I started to thank him for the ride.

"No need," he said, once again gazing at Great-Grammie.

He watched us pick up our things and head up a narrow, rocky, well-worn path to the road, then said, almost to himself, "My Grammie always said that if the island is in your blood, it will call you back home."

I turned and stared at him, so I know he watched us until we reached the top of the rocky hill. We turned to wave one last time and then he climbed back into his boat and putt-putted back to the shore where we'd found him.

Chapter 36

Sand and pebbles slipped beneath our feet as we scrambled up the path toward the road that would lead us to the town of Deer Isle. Great-Grammie kept putting her head up into the air and sniffing like a dog. I understood why. The salt air was so fresh and tingly and the sea roses that lined our path filled the air with sweet flower smells.

The sun was still pretty high in the sky and it was a hot day, which meant that there were little patches of liquid tar on the road. As we hiked along, our Keds now and then would stick for a moment, almost as though the road was warning us not to hurry. Chris and I looked from side to side curiously, but Great-Grammie stared straight ahead, and her footsteps led the way.

Do you know the movie *Wizard of Oz*? I remembered that movie as we hiked along. The four of us—if you include Elizabeth, the doll baby—were on our own road to adventure, except we weren't following a yellow brick road, but an old asphalt road full of potholes. Still, like Dorothy, the Tin Man, the Scarecrow, and the Cowardly Lion, we were all bound for some kind of wisdom—in our case, though, we were heading to a little white farmhouse instead of the Emerald City.

The village of Deer Isle looks like a toy town that you'd put beside a model train track. Small and cute, its miniature one- and two-story buildings hug the road. We read signs for a post office, grocery store, newsstand, real estate/law office, reading room, and several other businesses. I looked longingly at the ice-cream sign in the window of a gray-shingled grocery that tilted toward the sea, but I knew that we should save the $1.27 for emergencies.

Great-Grammie had said nothing since she climbed into the boat, but she set the pace for our march to Knowlton Lane. She held her head up high in the warm breeze and it caressed her face like a mother's hand would glide softly across her baby's cheeks. It seemed to me that she had a compass inside her. She never once glanced at any landmark beside the road, but set her face homeward, with her doll pointing in the same direction, nestled right under her chin, wrapped in her arms.

My arms were already sore from lugging my bookbag, so I struggled to keep up. I wondered how Chris was managing with our heavy suitcase and his bag, but I didn't ask. It felt as though we were part of a church processional and you never talk or even whisper when you're in one of those. I spent my time wondering what we'd find at the end of our hike.

We lost sight of the ocean after we passed a pretty red barn-like hotel called the Pilgrim Inn.

"Do you think Pilgrims vacationed here?" Chris joked.

Those were the first words he'd said since we started walking. At last, quite a ways outside of town, we stopped to rest on a big rock beside the road. I had to run ahead and grasp Great-

Grammie's arm to get her to stop for a minute. I handed her a bottle of water and I handed Chris an apple.

"How much farther do you think it is, Chris?" I whispered.

"About another two miles or so," he answered, after consulting my notebook for the ten thousandth time that day.

We were stretching our arms and staring idly at the nearby white farmhouse with black shutters and pretty vegetable and flower gardens when a battered old pickup truck bumped into view and moaned to a stop beside us, the motor still chug-chug-chugging.

"Can I help you?" the man asked, glancing at us, then staring at Great-Grammie.

I wanted to say no, thank you, because I remembered the thousands of times my parents had warned me never to speak to strangers, but Chris walked up to the open window and said, "We'd appreciate a ride, sir, if you're going our way."

"Where to?" the man asked.

"Knowlton Lane, Sunset."

"Knowlton Lane is it? Hop in." The driver, who was middle-aged and had a stubbly chin, was chewing on a toothpick. Suspenders held up his work clothes and his pant legs disappeared into rubber boots. He climbed out of the truck, lifted down the tailgate for Chris and me, then opened the passenger door and tried to help Great-Grammie onto the passenger seat. She backed away quickly, dropping her doll and putting her hands behind her back.

"No! Let's take the horse, Erolyn," she insisted.

Was she afraid? Or was she remembering old warnings about strangers that she, too, had once heard?

"Christopher? Do you think it's a good idea to take a ride from a stranger?" I hissed urgently.

He nodded, his eyes on the man.

The driver looked curiously at Chris and me, and Chris explained, "Great-Grammie's just a little confused, sir. It's been a very long time since she's been home."

"Home?" the man asked, taking the toothpick out of his mouth.

"We're bringing her to the farm where she grew up."

The man peered at Great-Grammie again and asked, "Is she a Small or a Knowlton?"

"How did you know?" I asked, too surprised to remember not to talk to a stranger.

"The size and the eyes," he said.

Gee, Down Easters sure don't waste any words, I thought. "She's a Knowlton, but her mother was Sarah Small and she was pretty small, I guess," I told him.

"She was. And you've got her eyes," he said.

"I'm part Small myself," the man explained when he saw the surprise on my face.

Despite our coaxing, Great-Grammie refused to climb or be lifted, pushed, or pulled onto the seat of that old pickup.

"Maybe she'll think she's riding on a hay wagon if we put her on the back of the truck," Chris suggested.

Our driver and Chris hoisted Great-Grammie up on the back of the truckbed and I scrambled up on one side of her, with Christopher on the other.

"Hold her tight," the man warned.

Stretching out behind us was a small mountain of lobster traps and a very strong smell of fish.

The three of us thumped along, enjoying the unexpected ride with our legs dangling, a warm breeze swirling blowing, and the smell of fish wrapping itself around us. I knew that my parents wouldn't approve of any of this, but I'd already broken so many rules that riding on the back of a truck probably wouldn't be high on the list. Every now and then, Chris and I would exclaim and point when we saw a house, sign, or barn that had been described by Great-Aunt Elizabeth or pictured in her albums. The truck bumped and lurched and swerved to avoid potholes, and we slid and swerved with it, barely staying upright.

Suddenly, the truck stopped altogether and the driver leaned half his body out the truck window, looked back at Christopher, and shouted, "Knowlton Lane!

"Now where?" he yelled.

"To the old white Knowlton farmhouse across the lane from a tiny beach," Chris yelled back.

The lane veered crazily off to the right, nearly hidden under a canopy of trees. We held onto each other and the truckbed as the truck lurched down a hill. My heart was lurching almost as much!

Soon—but not soon enough for me—we pulled onto a long drive whose crushed-shell surface had sunk deep into the ground a long, long time ago. Weeds grew up amongst the sharp points of granite rocks that poked out of the drive. I'm sure our newly met relative was afraid he'd lose a tire if he drove any farther.

I turned my head quickly and saw the low, ancient white farmhouse with the two welcoming porches that had haunted my dreams for weeks. "One for company, one for family," Great-Aunt Elizabeth had explained.

"This is the place! At last!" I think I breathed those words to myself. Christopher reached for our bags as our driver reached for Great-Grammie while I jumped down.

When the old lady landed on her feet, turned, and saw her old home, she stood rooted in the road, her eyes wide open. A half dozen times she wiped her hands across her eyes and looked again. She swallowed hard, but she didn't say a word. Chris and I turned to thank our new friend.

"Anybody know you kids and Great-Grammie are here?" the man asked, his eyes on the old lady.

Pretty smart of him, I thought, but I'd prepared myself for this question.

"My grandparents will be coming soon," I told him in a voice that shook, with my fingers crossed behind my back. I hoped what I said was true. But he didn't seem to notice my shaky voice. He nodded, put the toothpick back in his mouth once again, and climbed back into the old battered pickup truck. Just before he pulled out of the driveway, he stuck his head out of the window, swiveled his toothpick to the corner of his mouth, and yelled, "If you need anything, ask anyone and they'll help you. Around these parts, we think highly of Knowltons."

I smiled and waved, turned to my great-grandmother, and saw tears pouring down the wrinkle rivers on her cheeks. Chris walked up silently and stood beside Great-Grammie and me.

Oh, how I hoped we'd done the right thing!

# Chapter 37

Knee-high daisies covered the field—it sure couldn't be called a lawn—and carpeted the orchard that stretched between us and the house. Chris and I picked up the bags and the two of us held Great-Grammie's hands as we headed toward the house, stumbling across the bumpy field. The closer I got to the ancient home that my ancestors had built and lived in, the bigger my heart puffed up, until my chest didn't seem big enough to hold it. I was having a hard time breathing and I could feel Great-Grammie's hand trembling. I squeezed it for comfort—though whether the comfort was for me or her, I wasn't sure just then.

To the right of the house, the gray clapboard barn seemed to be kneeling on the earth. The hollyhocks surrounding it were almost as tall as the sagging barn door. Beside the barn, an outhouse tilted toward the sun. The farmhouse looked just as it had in Great-Aunt Elizabeth's very old photographs, except the porches looked lonelier. An ancient—and empty—wooden chair rocked slowly on the front ("company") porch and I wondered if someone—maybe even a ghostly Knowlton—had been sitting there only a minute before we looked. Kind of a spooky feeling!

Just as Great-Aunt Elizabeth had said, a garden welcomed people to the porch that sheltered the kitchen door. A picket fence with crackly, peeling white paint guarded the tangle of flowers and weeds. We walked up to the gate, which sagged on one hinge. Then we hesitated.

"Anybody home?" I called weakly.

Christopher must not have seen the chair rocking, because he said in a very businesslike, non-scaredy-cat way, "Let's find the key. It's going to be dark soon."

The gate hesitated to invite strangers into the empty house. It squealed in protest when Chris pushed it open, but he didn't notice. He walked in long strides along the wavy brick walkway past a tangle of plants and up to the porch. I hesitated a minute, then pulled gently on my great-grandmother's hand. Like the first time I held it, I realized how hard and bony and bumpy and leathery it was—and how it was almost exactly the same size as my soft, pillowy hand.

"We're home, Erolyn," she breathed, without taking her eyes off the house.

Suddenly, when we reached the porch, she cried excitedly, "Mumma! Mumma!" Although the words sounded like a little girl's, the voice was cracked and creaky and old.

She stumbled onto the porch, which was covered in dust and old crinkled brown leaves, and tried to open the heavy, peeling dark green door. Cobwebs crisscrossed the top corners of the door, proving that it hadn't been opened for a long time.

"Mumma! Mumma! I'm here!" Great-Grammie called again and again as Christopher and I scrambled on our knees beside the three tilting, worn-down steps, running our hands under the splintery old boards as we tried to find the key. Thanks to Great-Grammie's cries and my excitement, guilt, and worries, the butterflies in my stomach were fluttering crazily.

I sat *plunk!* down on the ground with relief when Christopher finally called excitedly, "I've found it!"

We crowded together by the door as Christopher stuck the heavy, rusty key into the lock. He turned it one way.

No click.

He turned it the other way.

No click.

He turned it again, this time with two hands and pushed hard.

Finally we heard a tiny *snap!* and all three of us breathed out a breath we'd been holding the whole time.

CREEAAKK!

The door seemed sorry to let us see an empty kitchen without a mother or good cooking smells or a fire crick-crackling in the old iron stove, so it opened very slowly. Christopher had to put his shoulder to it and push hard. The three of us stood shoulder to shoulder, not quite sure what we'd find. I was afraid to look at Great-Grammie's eyes, experiencing the fear that I probably should have had three days before—the fear that I'd done something terribly wrong, that maybe grandparents really *do* know best.

No one moved or said anything. We were all wrapped in silence together. It was a quiet like I'd never heard before. The house seemed to be holding its breath, wondering who the strangers were. And we were holding our breaths, too, wondering what the house was holding. Or hiding.

Cautiously, Chris and I peeked in through the doorway.

Dust covered the floor. Cobwebs decorated the windows. But even still, there was a feeling of warmth and welcome that was odd—but I only realized that later. Very faint smells of long-gone flowers, Saturday suppers, baked cookies, and wood fires crept to our noses.

The kitchen walls were painted a bright, sunshiny yellow. Windows lined three sides of the big, airy room, flooding it with late afternoon light and showing us the colorful garden on the side, the barn and rose trellises in the back, and the ocean and early signs of sunset in the front. A big, black wood-burning stove stood next to a huge brick fireplace, with a pile of kindling stacked neatly between the two, as if the house had been anxiously waiting for company.

The sink was a big old nickel tub with a pump. Above it, a dishcloth dangled from a swing-out towel rack. A calendar with a picture of Quoddy lighthouse and the date May 1945 hung beside the bare window over the sink. On the window-sill, a blue-and-white flowerpot held the skeleton of a geranium. Yellowed linoleum covered the floor; it had peeled up in spots to reveal wide, dark-brown floorboards. Old ladderback chairs circled a huge oval table that sat on a hooked rug beside the door. The vase of dusty dried flowers in the center gave the place a feeling of welcome.

After wandering into the kitchen, we realized that Great-Grammie had stayed on the other side of the doorway, with a blank look on her face. We pulled her gently into her old home. Still feeling guilty—but not as scared—I peeked into her eyes and noticed that the window shades had been pulled down behind her eyeballs.

Curious to see what the rest of the house held, Christopher and I tiptoed into the parlor, as if we were afraid of awakening a ghost. I gently lowered Great-Grammie onto the couch. Chris quickly rolled up the dark green window shades; they clattered on their trip up the window. I wished the shades on Great-Grammie's eyes would roll away as easily!

Faded braided rugs covered the wide tipsy floorboards. Except for a large, polished wooden captain's chair, the furniture was black and silky, with wooden arms and legs. "Grampie has a chair like this—he says it's filled with horsehair!" Chris whispered. Over the couch, an odd round wreath framed in dark wood ringed the picture of a sleeping baby. Old books lined up stiff and straight on the bookshelf; a round brass ship's clock and two lanterns were anchored on the top. A blue-and-white bowl with dusty dried rose petals stood on one end table, surrounded by fancy gold frames holding tin pictures of brides, little kids, and old, bearded men. Benjamin Knowlton's 1865 discharge from the Twentieth Maine hung on one wall above a worn-looking sword. Nearby was a picture of Abraham Lincoln. A ship model sailed across the fireplace mantel.

"Gee, Chris, do you think that's the ship that sank with Great-Grammie's father?" I asked, walking up and peering at the tiny little strings, masts, lifeboats, and cannons.

We left Great-Grammie sitting on the horsehair sofa and continued our tour. A big, scarred table nearly filled the length of the dining room, with ladderback chairs lined up along the long sides, a captain's chair at one end, and a stuffed flowery chair at the other. Ship pictures filled these walls. Over the fireplace hung another sword and an old gun as long as I was tall.

"I wonder who used those?" Chris said, walking up to study them.

"Grammie said there were lots of wars and pirates and sea

battles around here," I reminded him. "Maybe these are from a battle!"

We didn't spend much time in the big downstairs bedroom and just peeked into the four little bedrooms upstairs, which were connected by a twisty-turny hallway. Every room had a wooden rope bed, braided or hooked rugs, a bureau, a washstand holding a pitcher and bowl for washing up, and a view of the sea. The windows were lit with the colors of the sinking sun.

"We'd better see about dinner before it gets too dark," Chris reminded me when I turned and picked up a dusty porcelain doll that had been sleeping in an ancient cradle.

I suddenly remembered how my stomach had been rumbling for the last couple of hours and I quickly returned the doll to its bed and followed him back down the stairs. As he passed Great-Grammie, Chris smiled into her empty eyes, then collected the living room's oil lamps on his way into the kitchen.

"Great-Aunt Elizabeth said Knowltons always keep food here," I reminded him, anticipating a delicious dinner. Then I realized with dismay that an eleven-year-old girl and twelve-year-old boy would be the chefs—and one of them was me!

After rummaging through cupboards and under cabinets, we decided on a menu of canned baked beans, canned peaches, and canned Spam. While Chris lit the kindling in the old stove, I peeked once again at Great-Grammie, who had begun to rock back and forth, back and forth. To my surprise, the song she was humming wasn't the nameless tune I knew so well. It was "Amazing Grace," a hymn we'd sung in church just last Sunday. This was the first connection I'd seen Great-Grammie make with the real life I knew in Maine during the summer of 1957.

"Great-Grammie? Great-Grammie?" I asked quietly, edging

226

closer, not sure whether I should interrupt or not. When she didn't open her eyes or stop rocking, I returned to the kitchen to gather plates and silverware as Chris worked on the fire.

After Chris had shown me how to prime the pump and get fresh water for drinking, I swept the floors and collected the cobwebs with a feather duster. Then I wandered out onto the porch and into the garden to take a closer look.

Weeds of all sizes and shapes had sprung up, but the flowering plants that had produced blooms for maybe two hundred years seemed to be holding their ground. I wondered which ones had sent baby plants to my grandmother's South Portland garden, and when I began wandering around, I recognized the bleeding heart and Solomon seal plants that looked just like hers. Covering the wavy brick walkway and every open patch of ground were sky-blue forget-me-nots, one of my favorite little flowers. I was surprised to discover two tomato plants hidden amongst the blooms and picked a big, ripe, red tomato to add to our feast.

"Betsy, I need your knife," Chris yelled, and I stopped my wandering and returned to the kitchen. By the time we'd pried the tin lids off the cans and sliced the tomato with my handy-dandy Swiss Army knife, long shadows were reaching the farmhouse. Christopher and I moved a little table onto the front porch. The three of us ate watching the sun send layered streaks of color over the tiny, rocky beach nestled between evergreens and boulders that stretched on the other side of Knowlton Lane.

Great-Grammie never said a word.

"I can see why they call this place Sunset," Chris suggested, leaning back in his chair when he couldn't fit another forkful of dinner into his mouth.

"Maybe we can find a shovel in the barn and try digging for pirate treasure tomorrow!" I said happily as we cleared the table and settled Great-Grammie back in the parlor.

"Betsy, have you forgotten why we came here?" Chris asked when we returned to the kitchen and started washing dishes with water he'd heated on the old stove. "We've got to figure out why Great-Grammie needed to come so badly. And we've got to do it pretty fast, before your grandparents either come or send someone to get us."

He was right—he was always right!—and my face got all red when I realized I'd been thinking of myself and my adventure instead of my great-grandmother and her adventure. By the time the dishes were washed and put away, darkness was beginning to cover the sky and Chris had lit the oil lamps in the kitchen. I'd never seen lamps like that used for light instead of decoration. It had never occurred to me that the old house wouldn't have electricity! Suddenly, I realized how helpless I would have been if Chris hadn't come with us. The thought hurt my stomach.

"What do we do now, Chris?" I asked, suddenly realizing that my Plan hadn't gone any farther than the door of the old farmhouse.

What had I been thinking back in South Portland? Did I expect Great-Grammie to regain her memory miraculously? That she would pull out a treasure map from under her girlhood bed? That she would find someone here she needed to talk to? Probably I'd been thinking all those things—but I sure hadn't anticipated what was happening now. Great-Grammie was sitting and rocking and not saying anything or looking for anything. And no one from the island seemed to be looking for her.

By the expression on his face, Chris didn't know what to

suggest, either, but he wouldn't admit it. I was kind of relieved about that because, after all, this was my Plan. Still, I was counting on him to do a lot of our thinking now.

"Let's get a good night's sleep and in the morning we'll decide what to do," he said in a strong voice after a minute.

I thought that sounded like a very grown-up idea, but I wasn't sure how to do that.

"Where should we sleep? I'm afraid Great-Grammie might try to run somewhere and we'll lose her in the dark," I said, hoping that he'd reassure me. I was a little afraid to crawl into one of those old beds in the tiny little bedrooms upstairs, too— though I would have died rather than admit that I was afraid to be alone in a room inside my ancestors' house.

Chris thought for a long minute, then decided that we'd sleep in the living room, Great-Grammie would sleep upstairs in one of the bedrooms, and we'd lock all the doors. That sounded reasonable.

I took a lantern in one hand and Great-Grammie's hand in my other hand, and she followed me upstairs, shuffling her feet and moving as if she was in a trance. Chris followed, carrying our suitcase.

"Which room was yours, Great-Grammie?" I asked.

She didn't answer me, but she moved straight into the little room at the very end of the hall. Chris left the bag and I heard him clattering down the bare wooden stairs. Before I could do much more than open the suitcase, he was back with a bucket of water, which he poured into the washstand.

How did he know to do all this old-fashioned stuff? I wondered as he headed back down the stairs.

I hesitated for a moment, and then I helped Great-Grammie out of her dress, shoes, and stockings, slipped her white nightgown over her head, and washed her face and hands like my mother used to do for me when I was little. I'd watched my Grammie unpin her mother's long braids and brush out her hair many times, so I knew what came next.

Chapter 38

Great-Grammie sat on the edge of the low, old-fashioned bed just like a sleepy little girl. I fumbled in her hair for the pins, carefully put them on the old wooden bureau, then unbraided the long braids and brushed and brushed her hair. Great-Grammie didn't say anything.

As I brushed, I thought about how a short time ago my great-grandmother had frightened me, how I'd been afraid of being with her, touching her, or wanting to know anything about her. How and when all those things had changed, I couldn't say. It had been so gradual. Suddenly I was overwhelmed with so much love for this tiny old lady who had somehow lost herself. She seemed to be trying so hard to find Edna just one more time. Just one more time!

I couldn't say that I knew her any better now than I had when I first saw her rocking in her tiny, dark bedroom on my first day in Maine, but I suddenly realized with a jolt that it didn't matter whether I knew what her favorite color was or how she felt about digging up pirate treasure. I had grown to

231

love her so much that somehow she had become a part of me and I had become part of her. Every stroke I pulled through her hair seemed to pull me back in time a little farther, until I guess I stopped thinking. I might have been anyone in a long line of caregivers in my family: mother, grandmother, great-grandmother, daughter, granddaughter, great-granddaughter. We were all one person right then, in the dark little bedroom nestled under the low roof of my family's ancient home.

I would probably have continued brushing her hair all night long, but I heard a log drop far away in the parlor and the noise brought me back to my own body and the year 1957. When I left the little bedroom, Great-Grammie was tucked into bed like a baby, with the stiff white sheets and old gray wool blanket folded neatly and pulled up to her chin. Her doll lay on the pillow next to her.

"Good night, Great-Grammie," I whispered, hoping she would look at me and see me just once as her great-granddaughter. I wished just once she'd see my long brown braids and the mahogany-colored eyes that looked just like hers. I wished that just once she'd call me by my real name and not the name of a long-dead sister.

I closed my eyes and held my breath and tried to wish her eyes into raising their window shades so we could at last get a clear look at each other. When I couldn't hold my breath any longer, I let the air out with a gasp and opened my eyes, hoping for some sign.

But there wasn't any.

I could tell by the gentle up-and-down of her chest that she was asleep. I quietly closed the door and tiptoed down the hallway. Before I creaked down the steps, I stopped for a minute in front of a tiny, wavy hall mirror.

Just to make sure that I really was still Elizabeth-called-Betsy.

* * *

When I returned to the parlor, I saw that Chris had been busy since I'd been gone. He'd rummaged around the kitchen again and found tins of food for breakfast, banked the kitchen fire in the stove, and started a fire in the parlor fireplace, gathered blankets from the downstairs bedroom, and lit just enough lamps to make the room look cheery. He'd pulled the couch over beside the fireplace and made up a bed there, then built a nest of blankets on the other side of the fireplace.

"I've locked the doors, Betsy," he started to say, but I quickly interrupted him.

"Christopher, I still think we did the right thing bringing Great-Grammie here, but I don't know why she had to come. She doesn't seem to be looking for anything and no one seems to be looking for her," I confessed in a rush.

"But she knows where she is—she called for her mother," he reminded me.

I hesitated, since this was my Plan, but I had to admit, "I don't know what to do next."

"My mother always says to see what the morning brings," Chris suggested, looking at me as though he was afraid I might start to cry or something.

Just because my mind was working so hard and I couldn't sleep, I started prowling through the parlor, hoping to find some sort of clue that would explain our trip. At the time, I thought I was trying to get clues to my Great-Grammie, but now I realize the clues I searched for were about me—clues about who I was, where I belonged, the people who were part of me.

I stared at a big photograph in a heavy gold frame. Six brothers stood behind seated parents and one sister. "Gee, they all look grumpy or sad," I murmured more to myself than to Christopher, but he nodded silently. I pulled books off the shelves and dusty, flat bouquets of pressed flowers slipped out of their dusty, yellowed pages. I wondered who had read those books and whose flowers they were and why they were important enough to save. I pulled open drawers that smelled of long-ago autumns and pawed through letters, pictures, news clippings, and children's art. Some of the names and faces looked familiar, but most didn't.

"Chris! Listen to this!" I called excitedly when I found the newspaper clipping describing my great-grandmother's wedding. I read out loud, *The bride is the Knowltons' much-loved only daughter and she will be sorely missed. But with Mr. and Mrs. Henley go all the island's blessings, best wishes, and hopes for a happy, healthy, prosperous future.*

The *Deer Isle Gazette* described how this very parlor had been banked in calla lilies and ivy for the ceremony. The paper described Great-Grammie's gown, listed the guests, complimented the foods they ate, and praised the cake the bride's mother had baked. "Grammie said my birthday cake was the same recipe her great-grandmother had used for Great-Grammie's wedding cake!" I reminded myself.

"Wow!" I whispered over and over again as I continued my tour of memories. Christopher said nothing—but perhaps I just forgot he was in the room after awhile.

It must have been late into the night when I closed the last drawer after peering at the last picture. Great-Aunt Elizabeth had said that this house could tell the whole story of my family. At that moment, I understood what she meant. But I still didn't think I'd found anything that could explain why Great-Grammie wanted to come here so badly.

Just then, the old ship's clock struck midnight and I jumped—I hadn't realized that Christopher had wound the old timekeeper. Actually, I had no idea of what he'd been doing all night. I turned to see him working on the fire. Chris pointed to the couch and I crawled into the nest of blankets there while he stuck another log into the fire. He poked at it for a while before he rolled onto his blanket bed, but he must have gone to sleep right away because his breathing got real slow and steady. I was glad, because he'd worked so hard.

But I couldn't sleep.

In my mind, I toured the whole house again, this time very slowly, looking in my memory for something that Great-Grammie might need to find. I thought about everything I'd done that very long day, from putting the note into the spice cabinet to rushing down Shawmut Street with Great-Grammie, discovering Chris by my suitcase, the frantic bike ride to the bus, the endless bus trip, the journey across the Reach, and the walk and ride to Sunset.

What made me think that I knew more about Great-Grammie than her own daughter?

I couldn't answer that question very well now. But if I were being truthful, I'd admit that I was having fun in an odd kind of way. I had knots in my stomach and a guilty feeling in my head, but for the first time in my life I'd been brave enough to act on something I believed in, to launch myself on my own adventure. That felt good.

But, then again, if I were *really* being truthful, I had to admit that I was a lot braver and smarter and happier when I had my best friend with me to help me think and act and decide things. I tried to imagine what this trip would have been like without Christopher. Then I *really* felt my stomach knot. For a few minutes, I even thought I'd throw up when I realized some of the things that could've happened to a ninety-three-year-old lady and an eleven-year-old girl off by themselves on a long trip. That *didn't* feel so good!

Why hadn't I thought about all those things before I went ahead with my Plan? I knew that Nancy Drew would have!

"Christopher, I know you can't hear me, but I just wanted you to know how grateful I am that you came. Thanks," I whispered to the mound of blankets that was breathing softly.

Finally, I fell asleep.

Long after my eyes closed, I dreamed that Great-Grammie flitted into the parlor. Dressed in her long white nightgown, she stood by the front window, staring out into the darkness.

Chapter 39

When I woke up, soon after the sun had woken up, I heard Christopher in the kitchen, poking kindling into the old black stove. Remembering too late that Great-Grammie had a talent for escaping, I dashed up the stairs and found to my relief that she was lying in bed staring up at the ceiling, watching the early morning rays of sunshine dance across the blank white plaster. Her sheets and blankets were as neatly folded as when I left her last night. I looked at her closely, but her eyes and expression seemed just as blank as the eyes and expression of the doll in her arms.

"Great-Grammie?" I asked, wondering what this day would mean to her.

She slowly, so slowly, ever so slowly turned her head and focused her eyes on me. After one of the longest minutes of my life, it seemed as though her eyes recognized me. And then she smiled a warm, *young* smile.

"Is Mumma in the garden gathering the flowers?" she asked.

I didn't know how to answer that question, so I changed the subject.

"Let's get up and eat breakfast!" I urged. "Christopher—I mean, Steve—will have it ready soon."

I helped her out of bed and into her clothes, then braided her hair. My earliest memory—the one where she and I are rocking side-by-side and I think she's my sister—came back to me that morning. Once again, time and people seemed all confused. I felt like a mother helping her little girl get ready for the day.

"We're here!" I announced from behind Great-Grammie as she shuffled into the kitchen holding her doll baby. The kitchen smelled good, but it was empty. Through the rusting screen door, I could see Chris standing in the garden tangle, motionless, shading his eyes and staring across the orchard.

When I opened the door, I could see that he'd been working hard weeding the vegetable/flower patch. I wondered what had caught his attention, so I turned in the same direction he was facing. In the midst of a cluster of trees, I could just make out an old iron fence that we must have passed yesterday afternoon without paying any attention to it.

"What are you looking at?" I asked.

My question seemed to bring him back from far away. He didn't answer me, but turned with a smile and said, "Corned beef hash for breakfast and more canned peaches. I can even offer you a fresh tomato if you'd like," he added with a grin, showing me what he'd found in the tangled garden.

As we headed back into the kitchen, he told me that Great-Grammie had spent some of the night prowling. "She opened the back door and walked outside," he said. I gasped and my heart started beating wildly.

"What did you do?"

"I thought she might need to use the outhouse, so I decided just to follow her and make sure she was all right," he said. "But all she did was stand in the garden and stare at the moon. She must have been outside in the moonlight at least an hour."

"Gee, Chris, I'm sorry I didn't wake up—and I'm so glad you did!" Pretty soon I'd have to start making a list of all the things he'd done for us, there were so many of them.

He scratched at the chicken pox spots on his arms and just shrugged. "With all the little kids in my house, you get used to listening for suspicious noises."

Food always tastes best when you're camping or outdoors and the night spent on the old couch counted as a camping trip, I decided. Breakfast that morning tasted better than any meal I could remember. The tiny woman barely touched her food while Chris and I kept sneaking glances at her. She looked different somehow. Maybe it was because of that strange thought I'd had in her bedroom, but it seemed to me that she was growing younger as I watched. Her cheeks had pink spots in them—I'd never seen pink on her before. The shadows of the kitchen hid most of her wrinkles, while her braids—I hadn't taken the time to pin them up on her head like my Grammie did every morning—made her look like a little girl again. The darkness didn't show the difference between white and light hair.

"Where's Mumma, Erolyn? Is she in the garden?" Edna asked me.

I didn't know what to say, but my grandmother's favorite answer to her mother's questions came out of my mouth. "Bye 'n' bye," I said.

Suddenly, as though a magnet was pulling her, Great-Grammie stood up, cradled her doll in her arms, and headed to the kitchen door. It didn't even squeak as she pushed it open and headed down the porch stairs. I thought she would search the garden for her mother, but she was making a beeline over the path of forget-me-nots, through the garden gate, and across the field of daisies toward that rusty old gate.

"Maybe she's remembered something at last, Chris!" I whispered excitedly as I ran quietly behind her with my best friend behind me. The garden gate squealed a protest as we followed her through it.

Some little voice inside me told me to watch Great-Grammie, but not to interrupt her. The tiny figure moved faster and faster across the daisy field, never stopping or looking right or left. Then, suddenly, she slowed down and stopped—as though she'd hit a glass wall.

I stopped several steps behind her and Chris must have stopped a couple of steps behind me. We watched her put her hand up flat in front of her. Then she started moving again, but much more slowly. As she did, I glanced beyond the ornate black fence and rusty gate that stood a stone's-throw away from the beach. Shocked, I realized that the fence surrounded a cluster of slate and granite gravestones overgrown with wild roses. Suddenly, I was filled with fears I hadn't felt on Meeting-house Hill, though I didn't know exactly what I was afraid of.

Great-Grammie's eyes were fixed on the old black gate. The name KNOWLTON was arched above it, carved in metal. A row of tall, sad-looking evergreens lined every side of the cemetery, standing guard. I wondered if their job was to keep people out. Or people in. I wanted us all to stay out—and I was surprised at my thoughts because Grammie had shown me this summer that cemeteries aren't scary places, but *visiting* places.

The tiny old lady tried hard to open the latch, but she

couldn't get it to budge. Chris moved past me, gently removed her hands, and wiggled the rusty handle. He worked hard to push the gate open. The grass had grown up and a granite rock had popped out of the ground at the threshold, so the job took him a minute or two. Great-Grammie stood patiently, taking no notice of us and never taking her eyes off the tall granite stone. When at last the gate opened wide enough, Chris stepped aside and she walked past him. Instead of her normal shuffling steps, Great-Grammie clutched Elizabeth tightly around the waist in her old leathery hands and held the doll out in front of her like a bride holding a bouquet.

Something inside my stomach tightened into a knot and I wanted to scream, "Don't go! Don't go!" But when I opened my mouth, no sound came out. My eyes turned to Chris pleadingly, and I saw that he'd been watching me with a solemn look on his face. I couldn't understand what that look meant—which surprised me because I thought I was pretty good at understanding my best friend's expressions.

Chris held the creaky old gate open for me like I was some kind of a lady in a movie and he was a gentleman, then we both trailed her into the little, lonely cemetery.

"Papa said the ocean lulls generations of Knowltons to sleep and now I understand what he meant," I whispered, glancing behind me at the nearby ocean waves lapping the shoreline. I didn't know if Chris heard until I saw him nod.

Great-Grammie tiptoed through the little graveyard, running her hands across tilting slate stones with dates that went back as far as 1775 and the Revolutionary War. Chris and I moved silently along behind her, reading every stone. All of them had Bible verses. Two of the oldest stones had angels carved into the top, above the name. One had a weeping willow tree. The fourth had a skull—that one made me jump. The gray gravestones that looked as though they were once rocks on the coast of Maine had dates starting in the 1790s. They told something about the person they stood for: "Revered wife, mother, grandmother," "Lost at sea," "Joyfully he returns to his heavenly father."

I was counting the names that began with the letter E until I reached the far side of the cemetery, where the stones were different—taller and all white, with the names outlined in lichens. "Christopher!" I whispered in surprise when I moved close enough to read them. My eyes felt as big as the tomatoes we'd found in the garden. "Look at the names and the dates!"

Four little stones stood for Knowlton babies who were all born in the 1870s and had all died within a year of their birth— one, the stone said, actually died at birth. Three taller stones listed the birth dates of one brother and two sisters—1862, 1866, 1869—but the death dates were all the same!

August 15, 1879.

When I walked a little closer, I could read the words on each grave:

STEPHEN STINSON KNOWLTON
Kind son, faithful friend, loving brother
The sea claims her own

EROLYN BUCKMINSTER KNOWLTON
The laughter in our home
Lost to us, but not to God

ELIZABETH ESTHER KNOWLTON
Sunshine has left our lives
Trust in the Lord with all your heart;
lean not upon your own understanding.

"No wonder Great-Grammie missed her brother and sisters so much—they all died the same day! What happened?" I turned to Christopher and tears were clouding my eyes. I'd never had brothers or sisters, but he did. His face was as white as the stones. He didn't look at me, just at the inscriptions.

I stood for a long time staring in shock at Erolyn's stone—the stone that covered the grave of the little girl my great-grandmother thought I was. Cold seemed to creep down my spine and through my bones. Was this what it would be like to look at your own grave I wondered?

Finally I moved on to the other two stones and I had the same strange feeling. After all, I knew another boy my great-grandmother had called Steve and an ancient doll that she had called Elizabeth.

That summer I never did figure out whether Great-Grammie could still remember how to read, but she didn't seem to need to read in this cemetery. Her knobby old hands moved over each stone and she seemed to greet them as friends. I heard her whisper, but I couldn't make out her words.

Christopher and I stood rooted to our spot in front of the white stones for a long time, watching the tiny old lady make her way through the cemetery. Mostly, we were lost in our own thoughts. The sounds of the sea—gentle lapping waves, the screech of seagulls, the breeze in the trees—were soothing. Bye and bye, after touring the whole cemetery and spending the longest time in front of the white stones, Great-Grammie sank down on the ground at the foot of the tall granite grave marker that just read "Knowlton."

Christopher took off his jacket and wrapped it around her shoulders. I ran back to the house and grabbed a blanket, so she wouldn't have to sit on the still-cold, damp ground. When

I leaned over Great-Grammie to wrap the blanket around her body, she put her hands on either side of my face and ran them down my cheeks. Startled, I looked into her eyes. To my surprise, it didn't look as though the shades were pulled down behind her eyeballs!

"Are you all right, Great-Grammie?" I whispered.

She just looked at me.

"Are you all right, Great-Grammie?" I tried again.

She smiled sweetly at me.

"Do you want us to sit here with you or do you want to be alone?" I asked in a whisper.

"Alone," she said, so softly that I had to lean my ear close to hear. As long as I was so close, I leaned over and kissed her on the cheek.

I'd never done that before, I realized with shock.

"I love you," she whispered to the wind as I pulled away, watching her.

"I love you, too, Great-Grammie," I said.

And I really, truly meant it.

Chapter 40

Once the tiny little woman was bundled, she closed her eyes with a sigh. Christopher and I stood in the cemetery awkwardly, knowing she'd given us permission to go, but not sure if we should. At last, I looked at Chris and he cocked his head toward the beach. We noiselessly left the cemetery. Christopher paused at the creaky old gate, hesitating to close it and disturb Great-Grammie's peace with its squeal. I knew because I could see the thoughts race across his face.

"Don't let's close it," I said. "We'll keep our eyes on her—she doesn't look as though she'll go anywhere right now."

He nodded. Without saying another word, we headed to the little beach, glancing back at the huddled figure in the cemetery now and then. For a while, we just sat on rocks in the sunshine, looking out at the empty horizon and thinking. At last, the gulls called out an invitation to play and we watched them swoop and dive. Seals glided in the sea not far offshore and I counted them, hoping they would swim in closer to us. In the back of my mind, I listened to the breath of wind that murmured as secretly as Great-Grammie had.

What was it trying to whisper to us? I wondered.

I think we both waited for the other one to say something—at least I know I did. When I couldn't stand the silence any longer, I said hesitantly, "Christopher, do you *really* think we should have come?"

Christopher stared out at the horizon for a long time before he dragged his eyes—and, I guess, his thoughts—back to me. He nodded. But he didn't say anything else.

I waited. And waited. And at last, when I couldn't wait any longer without bursting inside, I asked, "*Why* did she have to come so badly?"

Chris scratched at his chicken pox bumps and told me, "I think we'll learn the answer bye 'n' bye."

That was comforting—I knew that my lighthouse/friend wouldn't say anything he didn't mean. I hesitated for a minute because sometimes it's hard to say thank you, but I needed to. Badly.

"Chris, I can't thank you enough for all you've done for us. I thought I had a good Plan, but I know now that Great-Grammie and I would have been in big trouble if you hadn't come to help us."

He held up his hand to stop me from talking, but I kept going.

"I just want you to know, Chris, that I really, truly appreciate all you've done and I *promise* that I'll help you save up for your bike!"

He just looked embarrassed at those words—and he didn't look as though he knew what to say back. So, I stopped talking and tried to think of something else to do. I bent down, collected some flat stones, and started skipping them into the water.

"Storm's coming," he said after awhile, pointing to a curl of dark gray clouds that covered the ocean 'way off shore. The steel gray looked like it was moving slowly toward us. Once again, he scratched at his chicken pox spots; just watching him scratch made me want to scratch, too.

"We should get Great-Grammie," I said, turning to go.

"We can give her a few more minutes," he said, shading his eyes with his hand and staring out at sea.

I couldn't sit still one more minute. I ran up and down the little beach. Then I skipped all the flat rocks I could find on that little beach. I didn't want to face the thoughts that were dancing just behind my eyeballs in my head, so I paced up and down the beach, first with my hands behind my back and then swinging my arms. I ran up and down the tiny beach. I skipped up and down the tiny beach. I squatted down and hunted for sea glass. Every once in awhile I stopped to glance in the direction of the cemetery and then I peeked at my best friend, but he was just sitting on a flat-topped rock, staring out at the ocean, watching the clouds.

I wanted really, really badly to ask Christopher if he thought my grandparents would come for us. But I guess I was afraid of the answer—no matter what it would be.

And then suddenly we heard tires rumbling on the lane. At the same exact minute, both of us whipped our heads around to look. There it was—the old, gray Studebaker.

Chapter 41

Do you remember what it feels like on a hot day when a cold wave washes over you and you aren't expecting it? No matter how hot the day is, you feel all shivery on the outside and the inside at the same time.

Well, that's how I was feeling.

But, even though I was scared about what my grandparents would say to us and think of me, I was full of relief. Christopher had taken such good care of Great-Grammie and me, but I had begun to realize that this was too big a job for a twelve-year-old boy. We both needed someone to help us with the thinking.

I ran to the car before it even began to slow down. Papa jammed his foot on the brakes, I knew, because the car stopped with a jerk. His door, the passenger door, and a back door opened all at once.

"Betsy!"

"Betsy!"

"Betsy!"

Three very dear faces swam before my eyes: Grammie,

Papa, and Great-Aunt Elizabeth! They were all hugging me and talking at once.

"Are you all right? Is Great-Grammie all right?" they asked together, in a chorus.

I nodded and tried to smile, but I hugged all three of them really, really hard before I said, "We're all fine. Great-Grammie is asleep. Christopher is here with me! He found Great-Grammie and me and came with us and found the key and lit the stove and fireplace and cooked our food and weeded the garden and..."

I looked back for him and saw him walking slowly up to us, with his hands in his pockets and an embarrassed look on his face.

"I can't thank you enough, son, for taking care of our two very precious girls," Papa said, sticking out his hand, his arm still around my shoulder.

Before Christopher could shake it, though, Grammie had launched herself at him, wrapping her arms around his neck and hugging him. And Great-Aunt Elizabeth looked as though she was about to do the same.

After the hugging ended, the explaining started. I told them about buying the tickets, hiding the suitcase, finding Christopher by the tree, the frantic bike ride to the bus station, the two-bus trips, the walk, boat ride, and pickup that brought us to the old farmhouse.

When I stopped talking for a moment to catch my breath, Great-Aunt Elizabeth cried and wiped her eyes with her fancy lacy handkerchief and said, "We should have listened to you. We knew how much this trip meant to you all and we should have listened and brought you ourselves!"

I thought for a minute that Grammie would do and say something similar, but suddenly she admitted, "Now, knowing that you're all safe, I wouldn't have wanted to change anything that would have prevented you from having your great adventure! You've done nobly!" she added, her smile spreading from me to Christopher.

"But I have something to tell you." I decided that this was the right minute to be brave and honest at the same time. "We haven't been able to figure out why Great-Grammie wanted to come so badly! She hasn't said anything or done anything or searched for anything."

I hesitated, gasped another breath of air for courage, and admitted, "I guess you were right and I was wrong."

"Well, it's worth everything you've gone through to have the chance to get acquainted with the house of your ancestors and to understand why Great-Grammie loves it so much," Papa said soothingly, squeezing me to him. He looked over at Christopher and said, "Son, in awhile I'll head back to town and find a phone. We'll call your folks and tell them that you're fine and that we'll be home in another day or two."

Chris nodded and thanked Papa.

"Now, let's collect Great-Grammie, unpack our groceries, and have an old-fashioned lunch in an old-fashioned kitchen," Papa added. "I must admit, I'm starving and looking forward to a picnic!"

Great-Aunt Elizabeth and Grammie had already started toward the tiny cemetery, discussing the last time that they had visited the family's farmhouse as they walked. I raced to catch up and pass them by. When I reached the gate, I stopped running and tiptoed up to Great-Grammie so I wouldn't startle her when I woke her up. Meanwhile, Grammie and Great-Aunt Elizabeth had stopped to exclaim over the ocean of roses that had linked many of the gravestones with blooms.

"Almost like the bonds of family that connected them through the years," Great-Aunt Elizabeth marveled.

For a brief moment, I stood over my great-grandmother and marveled at how young she seemed to have become. Her little girl's body was curled like mine does when I'm reading a book on the floor. One braid was hanging down her chest, the other was behind her back. Her doll, Elizabeth, was cradled in her arm and cuddled under her cheek—and those cheeks looked pink and white, like the roses that twined around the cemetery. She had a sweet, sweet smile on her face—I hadn't seen her really smile like this before today, I realized. The look on her face was so peaceful that I hesitated to wake her up. But I knew she must be hungry and she'd be glad to see her company.

"Great-Grammie! We have company!" I whispered, but she didn't hear me, so I gently put my hand on her shoulder and bent lower to whisper the news again.

She lay so motionless that I got a little scared.

"Great-Grammie? Great-Grammie!" This time I spoke very clearly. Out of the corner of my eyes I could see Grammie and Great-Aunt Elizabeth turn their heads in my direction.

Edna Knowlton Henley didn't move.

"Grammie! Papa!" I screamed.

* * *

I'm not really sure what happened next. I remember plunking myself down on the ground next to that tiny body and wrapping my arms around her. I tried to rock her and hum to her just like she had done a million times to her doll baby, Elizabeth. I thought that maybe this was the way to get her to wake up.

I remember sobbing and pleading with her to open her eyes and look at me.

I remember looking up at a tangle of legs and feeling a tangle of arms trying to pull me away, but I'm not sure how that all happened because I was crying so hard that I couldn't see anything but tears.

The next thing I knew, Grammie had wrapped her arms around me so tightly that I could hardly breathe and Papa was picking Great-Grammie up in his big, strong arms very tenderly. He carried her across the field of daisies and over the pathway of forget-me-nots, then into the old Knowlton farmhouse as I stumbled behind, with Grammie's arms around me and Christopher walking beside me.

Raindrops began to fall just as we reached the garden gate.

Papa must have known which bedroom was Great-Grammie's because he carried her up the stairs and down the twisty-turny hall to the little bedroom at the very end. Great-Aunt Elizabeth pulled back the stiff white sheets that I had smoothed earlier that morning and Papa laid my great-grandmother, who had thought I was her sister, on the bed. Edna's daughter pulled the sheets up over the little old body and folded them under her chin, just as if she'd been a little girl taking a morning nap.

* * *

"It's my fault! It's my fault! It's all my fault!" I sobbed, sitting on a chair in the kitchen as Christopher lit a fire and kept glancing at me. I felt as if my heart had cracked and broken into ten million tiny pieces. I couldn't stop the tears from rolling down my cheeks.

Warm, soft arms wrapped around me and rocked me, rocked me, rocked me just as though I'd been a baby, until at last the tide of salty tears turned to a trickle.

"There, there, there," Grammie murmured those words over and over and over again. Somewhere in the back of my mind, I wondered how many generations of kids in my family had been

253

comforted by that wonderful, soothing, meaningless word repeated over and over again. I know that somehow, just a little bit, the words were beginning to comfort me.

"I killed Great-Grammie!" I confessed at last, sitting upright. And my tears threatened to start all over again. Somehow, through the watery blur, I could see Christopher's legs in the corner of the parlor, but I didn't dare look at his face.

"You did nothing of the sort," Grammie said soothingly, pushing back my damp hair and wiping my eyes with a lace handkerchief she had borrowed from Great-Aunt Elizabeth.

"This wouldn't have happened if I'd listened to you!" I said defiantly, ready to assume responsibility for my Plan—and feeling so very, wretchedly miserable.

Suddenly, Great-Aunt Elizabeth swam through my tears into view. She knelt at my knees, grabbed hold of my hands, and said quietly, "Perhaps—just perhaps—that's true, Betsy. But, you see, you were wiser than all the grown-ups in our family. You understood our mother in a way that we didn't. You heard her heart-wish. So did we—we couldn't help but knowing that she longed to come home. But you heard it, and you listened to it, understood it, and *acted* on it."

When I looked at her and opened my mouth to ask a question, she added, "You gave her the greatest gift she's received in many a year. She wished with all her heart to cross the Reach once more, to return to her own people and her home because she wanted to die here. Thanks to you, her wish came true."

"I don't want her to die!" I started to cry all over again.

"But it was her time to go, Betsy," Grammie said, running her hand softly down my cheek.

"You made the end of her journey a happy one."

Chapter 42

Just hearing the *D* word made me start to cry again, but I still had too many questions to ask.

"If you knew she wanted to come here, why didn't *you* bring her?" I know my voice must have sounded angry.

Grammie looked at Great-Aunt Elizabeth, sighed, and explained.

"Many years ago, on a day very much like this one, when Edna was a young girl, she dared her brothers and sisters to a sailing race." Grammie's eyes left mine and she turned to look out the window a very long time before she continued. I wondered why she was telling me a sailing story. I glanced at Christopher and noticed that he was listening closely.

"Stephen took Elizabeth in his sailboat. Erolyn and Edna were each in their own boats. They set off around the point and they were having a *wonderful* time, laughing, teasing, using all their best sailing skills—and these were very skilled young sailors. But a storm came up suddenly from the northeast when they were far from shore. Edna was out in front and for several moments she didn't see what was happening behind her."

When Grammie swallowed and hesitated a moment too long, my great-aunt took over the story.

"Erolyn's sailboat capsized when she tried to turn it about too quickly," Great-Aunt Elizabeth continued. "She was the weakest swimmer of the four children and Steve knew that, so he dove into the water to rescue her when he saw her struggling in the waves.

"At that moment, Edna turned her head to shout a warning to her brother and sisters about the storm, to urge them to head inland. She saw what was happening," my great-aunt said. She explained that Edna had tried to turn her sailboat and reach them in time to help.

"Erolyn's swamped sailboat was broadsided by a big wave and the mast hit Steve on his head. Erolyn drowned trying to save him," Great-Aunt Elizabeth explained softly. "Elizabeth jumped into the water to find them, and she, too, drowned."

Edna's help came too late.

"Mama never forgave herself for challenging them to the race and then for failing to save them," Grammie said in a hoarse whisper. "For the rest of her life, she had terrible nightmares. I remember her waking up and sobbing—time after time after time...."

"So, you see, Betsy, we were afraid that coming home would unearth all those old horrors for Mama," Great-Aunt Elizabeth said gently. "We didn't understand what you could see so clearly—that Edna was ready to reach her brother and sisters this time, one last time, so they could all be together again. Forever."

* * *

I remember looking at Christopher when they finished telling the story and I realized how my Plan had taken such a huge and scary turn. I realized that if I'd heard that story earlier, I would never have been brave enough—or stupid enough—to bring Great-Grammie home to Sunset.

I remember that my best friend's face was as white as mine must have been.

I remember being tucked into bed in an upstairs bedroom much later, while my Great-Aunt Elizabeth rocked softly in an ancient, creaky rocker, watching over me. She was humming the nameless tune her mother had so often hummed.

I remember a cluster of people in black all gathered in and around the tiny little Knowlton cemetery that ran wild with pink and white roses. Most of them were people I'd never met before but somehow knew, thanks to their "eyes and size," as our friendly chauffeur had pointed out. He was there, too, by the way, standing in the back row next to our yellow-headed captain.

I remember watching the old wooden casket gently lowered into the ground and covered with rose petals before the men in my family—including Christopher—covered it with the black, rocky dirt of Great-Grammie's home.

I remember hearing someone whisper that my great-grand-father, Frederick Henley, would make one final voyage to Deer Isle. One of our Knowlton relatives had offered to sail Frederick's remains from Meetinghouse Hill to Sunset. "It seems only fair—after all, she went to his home for so many years," a tiny Knowlton cousin whispered to her daughter after the funeral ceremony ended.

I remember my best friend standing beside me silently wherever I was.

And the next thing I remember is Grammie feeling my forehead, inspecting my face, neck, and arms, and asking, "Betsy, have you ever had chicken pox?"

When I shook my head, thinking that was the right answer, she sighed.

Chapter 43

Last summer my vacation ran three weeks longer than any other student's at Ralph Waldo Emerson Elementary School in Chicago, thanks to the chicken pox, which covered my body like a very itchy, irritating blanket. I finally got my wish—Mom and Daddy both came to Maine to spend time with Grammie and Papa and me. And Christopher, too, of course. When I woke up in my bed on Shawmut Street and saw them walking through the doorway, the tears that I thought were used all up started all over again.

Over the next couple of days, I told Mom and Daddy everything: about being afraid of Great-Grammie when I first arrived, about the gang of five, the lighthouse-solid best friend, the treasure hunt, the adventure in Mr. Macomb's garden, the Plan, the wild bike ride, the bus trip, crossing the Reach, the journey to the ancient farmhouse, and the cemetery.

"I thought that if I could find buried treasure here in Maine, then you wouldn't leave me any more," I told them and watched my mother wipe her hands across her eyes.

"Betsy, you *did* find treasure in Maine—far, far more valuable than anything your mother or I will ever discover on our digs," Daddy told me with a serious look on his face. It took me awhile to understand what he meant.

You see, last summer I discovered that I had a heart that really worked. I discovered a treasure trove of love within my family—even in some people I'd never heard of before I arrived in Maine. I discovered friendships I hope I'll treasure all my life. And I found a best friend while digging for pirate loot on the beach.

But, instead of digging up buried treasure, we buried a great treasure.

On the beautiful island across the Reach.

About the Story

Whether we write fiction or nonfiction, writers draw on personal experiences and rely on people we know to help us flesh out a story. That is exceptionally true in the case of *Across the Reach*. These people are my people; their stories are my heritage; their homes are my home; their state has been my family's homeland for either nine or eleven generations, depending on which family line I trace. Everything in this book is so interwoven into my being that it is sometimes difficult to tell what really happened and what might very well have happened. The settings and the characters are all real, with a few erasures and additions.

The descriptions, personalities, relationships, and speech patterns for all the book's main characters are completely true. There has been a strong tradition in my family of naming daughters Elizabeth; my daughter is at least the fifth Elizabeth Henley in our family. Although I am the main character, I borrowed my sister Betsy's name and conveniently "disposed of" three younger sisters to create a lonely only child who needed to discover the power of relationships. I also changed my age for the convenience of the story; I decided it would be more believable to have two children run away with an elderly lady in the *Leave It To Beaver* days of the 1950s than during the Cold War years of the 1960s.

My grandparents play themselves in the book. The loving, ramrod-straight, *Pirates of Penzance*–playing grandfather with Algonquin ancestors is the Papa who invited me to play duets when I was very little. In her early years, my grandmother was always photographed on the ridgepole of barns, climbing granite cliffs, or preparing to dive into icy waters. In later years she loved to garden, and her plants (as are my mother's and some of my plants) really were rooted—literally and figuratively—in her ancestors' gardens. Esther had many kitchen specialties, but her seventeen grandchildren longingly remember her baked beans, molasses cookies, and strawberry pies. Unfortunately for us, she seldom used recipes, relying on the "feel" of the dough to know when it was precisely perfect.

Across the Reach focuses on Edna Knowlton Henley, my great-grandmother, who started losing her memory shortly after her husband, Frederick, died. In the days when I was a girl, people referred to her illness as senility; later, medical professionals would begin to speak of Alzheimer's. The details of my great-grandmother's early life are all accurate; she was born in the white farmhouse in Sunset to Henry and Sarah Small Knowlton and was courted by a man whose ancestors had lived on islands to the south of Deer Isle, in the Casco Bay. In her nineties, Great-Grammie really did try running home to Sunset—many times; the local policemen knew her well. As a very little girl, I woke up one night to discover my great-grandmother, dressed in a billowy white nightie, trying to pirate a motorboat in Mr. Sullivan's driveway. In fact, my editor asked me to tame down some of my memories, thinking that readers would never believe the true stories. She was quite a woman— and a remarkable athlete, even very late in life!

Readers who know South Portland and Deer Isle will recognize the landmarks, though the bridge to Portland has been replaced and houses have sprung up around my special cove at the end of Willard Beach. At my mother's suggestion, I moved my grandparents from their home on Davis Street to the land that was once the Henley family compound on Shawmut Street; those houses had all been demolished to make way for World War II shipyards, but the Ferry Village spot has remained special in my family's stories.

"I wonder what would have happened if we had taken Grammie Henley back across the Reach?"

My mother's half-whispered musing is what launched this story. *Across the Reach* tells the story that I *wish* had happened. And that is the beauty of writing—we can borrow from our past and change our future with the flick of a pen or the clatter of a keyboard!

Reading Between the Lines

1. Authors carefully choose **book titles**. *Across the Reach* is a literal title—the children take Great-Grammie Henley across Eggemoggin Reach. But the title is also symbolic. What is another type of crossing Elizabeth does?

2. **Leads** or beginnings to stories are crucial. Can you think of two other ways the author could have begun the book?

3. We relate best to **characters** who are well-rounded, with strengths and weaknesses. List the strengths and weaknesses of Elizabeth, Christopher, Grammie, Papa, and what you learn about Great-Grammie. Do you like the characters? Whom do you relate to the best? Why?

4. We all want to have a special **best friend**. How are Christopher and his family members and home very different from Betsy's other friends? What makes someone a best friend?

5. Elizabeth learns that **people** are not always how they first appear. Mr. Macomb, the "Gang of 5," Great-Grammie, and even Grammie all have unique stories, and the stories show someone very different from what Betsy sees on the outside. What are their "back stories"? What are your special stories that might make you different on the inside from what people see on the outside?

6. **Setting** is an important element in this story—and setting means **time** as well as **place.** Elizabeth tells us the year is 1957. How many activities and things can you identify that are different from the things you do and use today?

Details rooted in time are important when you're writing about another period of time. Are there details that surprised you? Appliances, books, or activities that you thought they should have—or were surprised they didn't have?

Research—even into the tiniest details of a book—is important. Authors want every detail to ring true to the time period. For example, originally, I wanted Great-Aunt Elizabeth to give Betsy a Barbie doll for her birthday because when I was eleven, my Great-Aunt Elizabeth gave me a red-headed Barbie. When I researched the doll, however, I learned that it was first introduced to the public 18 months after Elizabeth's eleventh birthday, so I had to eliminate Barbie—much to my regret. All of Betsy's treasures were available to children in 1957. The Girl Scout cookies she mentions selling have been sold for eighty years. Marshmallow Fluff, which makes marvelous fluff-ernutter sandwiches, has been manufactured in Lynn, Massachusetts, for seventy-five years. Alfred Hitchcock movies were the epitome of scary screen fare; the director produced his first horror movie in 1923.

7. **Place** is crucial to the story. Betsy lives far away from the coast of Maine and finds many traditions, daily rituals, and even the speech different from what is familiar to her. Describe the landscape of South Portland, where her grandparents live, and the landscape of Deer Isle. What details are similar—or very different—from where you live?

8. We all have a special place in our hearts; sometimes it's a real place, sometimes an imaginary place. The Knowlton farm in Sunset was Great-Grammie's **place of the heart.** List the characteristics of the farm that give you feelings, either positive or negative. What is your special place? What does it look like, smell like, feel like, taste like, and what sounds are there?

9. The **theme** is the heart of the story, the "heart message," or the main idea. *Across the Reach* has a number of themes. What are they?

10. One of the most important **themes** is stated in the very beginning of the book. What is it? Why would the author choose to do that? Can you write another beginning for the book?

11. **Seeing life** through another's eyes is one of the book's themes. Toward the end of the book, Elizabeth sits with Great-Grammie and begins to understand her better. What does she learn and feel? Have you ever tried to see the world through another person's eyes? When? How? What happened?

12. The definition of a **story** is that something has to happen (which you could call *conflict* or *problems*) and someone has to change. A book usually has several conflicts and some pretty big changes. What are the **conflicts** in *Across the Reach*? What **changes** take place? Who will never be the same again?

13. The **rhythm** of a story looks something like a heart monitor. You might also think of it as a mountain to climb. When a problem or conflict arises, the reader's heart beats faster. Can you draw a heart monitor, or mountain, for the story that shows what events help move the story along, what events make our hearts beat faster, and what is the peak event, when excitement and worry are at the highest point of the mountain? Where does the book end? At the top of the mountain? Part way down the mountain? Or at the base?

14. Books can have several different **endings**. Did you expect the ending of *Across the Reach*? How did it make you feel? Can you write two alternative endings to the book?

15. **Death** is a difficult topic. It can be very frightening,

or it can give a family a sense of peace. How did you feel about it? How do you think Betsy's family felt about it?

16. Like hikers in a strange area—or Hansel and Gretel—writers often leave clues about the journey on which they're taking their readers. Did you notice any **clues** about the ending that were planted earlier in the book? If you go back and look, you should find quite a few. What are they?